Cat-and-mouse games between a college student and a cop start out as *just sex*, with no strings, but gradually become more intense as the two men's relationship shifts and deepens.

Owned by the Cop
Copyright © 2019 Roland Graeme
ISBN: 978-1-4874-2591-3
Cover art by Martine Jardin

Published by eXtasy Books Inc or
Devine Destinies, an imprint of eXtasy Books Inc

Look for us online at:
www.eXtasybooks.com or www.devinedestinies.com

Owned by the Cop

By

Roland Graeme

CHAPTER ONE: RESTLESS NIGHT

L ife could be strange in its unpredictability.

Before he met his cop lover, Cordero Tejera was just another average, promiscuous young gay guy, going about his business. He harmed no one, and—somewhat ironically, as things turned out—he made a point of staying out of trouble with the law. A lot of good that did him!

Cordero was at home on a weekday night, and he was faced with one of those agonizing decisions a young gay man sometimes has to make. Should he stay at home and just jerk off, or should he go out in hopes of meeting somebody?

The convenience of staying in, and the odds against encountering the man of his dreams in a gay bar on a Wednesday night, at first tempted him to make an early night of it— alone. Cordero could give himself a quick self-induced orgasm with his fist and then fall asleep, all right there in his own comfortable bed.

He was actually undressed and in bed, with his laptop open beside him, ready to watch some internet porn to inspire a jerkoff session, when—perversely—the idea of going out began to appeal to him more and more. After all, one of Cordero's favorite taverns was right there in his neighborhood, within walking distance. It was one of the city's gay bars, which he frequently patronized, although usually on weekend nights.

He began to bargain with himself.

Just one drink. That was what Cordero promised himself, after a glance at the digital display of the alarm clock beside his bed. It was already close to midnight. *One drink, and then I'll come right home. I can jack off then. What's the harm?* He closed the laptop, and he got out of bed, his cock already twitching with the first signs of excitement.

He was already experiencing the tiny thrill of doing something which might be considered naughty and irresponsible. He had to get up and go to work in the morning, and he suspected that he'd end up breaking his own rule by staying at the bar for more than *one drink*.

Logic suggested that, because he wasn't really going out with the intention of trying to pick up somebody, it didn't matter much what he wore on this little excursion. But, at that moment, Cordero was thinking less in terms of logic, and more in terms of lust, by the minute. He decided that he ought to wear something which proclaimed his availability. After all, a guy never knew when he might get lucky!

On impulse, Cordero opened the top drawer of his bureau, where he kept a few clothes and personal items, but which also tended to be a quick-access repository for assorted sexual accessories — a jockstrap, an extra box of condoms and tube of lubricant, a pair of nipple clamps, a butt plug, a dildo, a dog collar, and so forth. Cordero rummaged through the clutter until he found what he was looking for.

The object was a cock ring. Cordero couldn't remember the last time he'd worn it — probably on some occasion when he'd hooked up with a guy who was into some light leather action. Unfortunately, Cordero's actual experience with leather sex, as opposed to fantasies, was limited to dressing up in vaguely *motorcycle punk* attire to go out, and then stripping down again and engaging what would have to be described as roughhousing with his hookup. He sighed, wishing he could go farther. Still, he had a few of the appropriate accessories, in the meanwhile. The ring was a single piece of heavy-gauge stainless steel, bent into a perfect circle and welded together at the seam, where the result was a slight ridge, almost like a traffic bump.

Holding the cock ring up to the light to examine it more closely, Cordero remembered that he preferred the way it felt to the sensation he got from the adjustable, snap-on kind. It happened to fit his genitals perfectly when he was fully erect, with just enough snugness to keep him continuously aware of its presence, surrounding his junk. He did recall, though, that the device tended to chafe him after he'd worn it for an hour or two.

So he went into the bathroom, where he rubbed a light coating of baby oil on the ring. Watching himself in the full-length mirror on one wall, he slipped the ring on, inserting one testicle through the circle at a time, and then tucking the head of his flaccid penis down to push it through, next.

Cordero pulled his dick away from his body so that he could push the cock ring down around the very base of his shaft, and he tugged on his balls as well, until the restraint was caught firmly around his perineum muscle.

He played with himself quite matter-of-factly with his oily fingertips, coaxing his prick into semi-erection. The cock ring seemed tighter than he remembered, and he grinned at his reflection, knowing that his cock and balls couldn't possibly have grown any larger!

But they were exceptionally turgid tonight, as a result of his horniness, his manipulation of himself, and the pressure exerted by the ring. He turned sideways to inspect himself in the mirror. Satisfied with the way the cock ring made his penis arc out away from his groin, lifting his nuts on either side of the bloated shaft, he washed his hands and went back into the bedroom.

He dressed quickly, in minimal clothing—his most comfortable jeans, the denim worn so soft by repeated washings that the material wasn't confining even though it stretched itself taut over his crotch, ass, and thighs.

He hadn't bothered to put on any underwear. He was in the mood to go commando. He dispensed with a belt, too. He really didn't need one to hold up those snug-fitting jeans. The waistband hugged his narrow waist and flat gut, with his hard-earned abs, and his buttocks did all the work of holding up the jeans. He did without socks, too—he just slipped on a pair of running shoes, so that his bare ankles provided a hint of nudity.

In fact, Cordero almost hated to take along his wallet for fear it would break the line of his body below the waist. He could just drop his keys into one front pocket, and a few folded bills in the other. But then he relented, shoving his wallet in front with his keys, but placing two condoms in his left rear pocket, where their outline was faintly discernible through the thin denim—making him a walking advertisement for sex.

Finally, he pulled on what he thought of as his *whore shirt*, because it was the sort of thing that only a male prostitute working the streets would wear outside of a gym. It was a string tank top, olive drab cotton, which for all practical purposes sheathed his torso only from the lower curve of his pectorals on down.

If Cordero squared his shoulders or flexed his arms suddenly, one or both of his nipples tended to pop out of the tank top. It was actually more sexually suggestive than walking around stripped to the waist could ever be, because it teased the observer. Luckily, he had the kind of shoulder and chest development which enabled him to carry off the provocative display.

Walking to the bar in the warm, dry night air, Cordero *felt* naked underneath his few clothes. He'd forgotten how the cock ring brushed against his inner thighs when he strode too energetically, and how sensitive it made his cock and balls feel, pushed up to form a high, protruding lump like that.

Hell, Cordero could even feel the bump of the ring's weld, where its ends had been closed during manufacture, pressing against his scrotum on one side! Excited, he could feel himself getting hornier, more reckless, more eager for sex, with each step he took.

He was on the prowl.

Chapter Two: Chauffeured

U pon his arrival at the bar, Cordero was surprised to see that it was two-for-one night. A customer could get both drinks at once, or get one plus a poker chip which could be redeemed later for a refill. Cordero's evenings out on school nights had become so infrequent lately that he'd lost track of such things.

He ordered bottled beer from the burly young bartender, whose name was Marc.

"I'll have to see some ID."

"ID? Come on, Marc," Cordero whined. "You know me. I come in here all the time."

"Yeah, and every time you come in, I ask you for ID. You know the drill. What I *don't* know is when one of those guys from the state liquor authority may decide to wander in here — and flash his badge. If he thinks I'm slacking off, going easy on guys who look underage, then it'll be my ass in a sling. And I don't mean in a fun way." Marc grinned. "It's not my fault you've got that baby face," he said to Cordero with a teasing tone.

"Shit," Cordero grumbled. But he pulled out his driver's license.

"Okay, college boy. One nice cold beer, coming right up."

"For giving me such a hard time, I ought to stiff you on the tip." But he did tip Marc, whom he liked.

Cordero couldn't help sulking a bit, as he carried his chilled beer bottle across the barroom, looking for a good spot to stand and cruise.

The drinking age was twenty-one, and he had, in fact, turned twenty-two a few months previously. He couldn't help it that he looked a bit younger. He was in his sophomore year at a local college and working part time. He felt reasonably independent and grown-up.

Cordero was athletic, good at swimming and soccer. He liked to build up his body by pumping iron at the gym on the campus. He had a muscular physique, which rather contradicted the impression created by the *baby face* Marc had mentioned.

Gay men presumably were obsessed by youth, with mature men attracted to younger sex partners. Cordero supposed his fresh-faced, boyish appearance had a certain appeal. But he desperately wished he was a little older — more manly. He wasn't all that attracted to guys his own age. He lusted after men in their late twenties or thirties, who were masculine-looking and masculine-acting. Cordero could even get aroused by the sight of a well-preserved hot daddy type in his forties or fifties. He might not even turn down a foxy number in his sixties! He didn't discriminate, except for the fact that he had no interest in effeminate guys.

He was deliberately negligent about shaving, and he flattered himself that the peach-fuzz beard stubble on his upper lip, chin, and cheeks made him look more mature.

He hadn't been sexually active for very long. But leaving his home town, and moving to this nearby community to attend school, had given his sex life a booster shot. Cordero was making up for lost time. He'd had casual flings with some of his fellow students, and even with a couple of his professors. There was another *older guy*, as Cordero thought of him — a senior citizen who was all of thirty-five — who lived in the town. His name was Riley. He was a rough-hewn working-class stud, a garage mechanic, and Cordero enjoyed having him as a casual fuck buddy.

As a result of these liaisons, Cordero thought of himself as quite the young gay blade about town. For example, there he was, in a gay bar, on the prowl, open to the possibility of hooking up with some stranger for some hot recreational sex.

He drank his beer, and he made eye contact with a couple of likely prospects. Some of his friends were there, and he touched bases with them, catching up. Their lives seemed more interesting than his—at least as they told it!

An hour had passed, and Cordero had just ordered his second pair of beers from Marc, when he was approached, quite boldly, by a guy who was the epitome of a metrosexual clone. He was a short fucker, with a tight, hard-muscled little body, an expensive haircut, a neatly trimmed mustache, and diamond studs set in his pierced earlobes. He was dressed as though he'd just come from modeling for a fashion shoot. The clothes were supposedly *casual*, but Cordero could tell the dude was carrying around over a thousand dollars on his back—not counting his ostentatious wristwatch, one of those multifunctional contraptions which probably required an engineering degree to operate.

There wasn't anything subtle or indirect about his come-on to Cordero. The man came right up to Cordero, and without so much as a greeting or a by-your-leave, he began groping him.

"Nice set of pecs." The short dude muttered under his breath as he slipped his hand beneath Cordero's tank top and massaged his chest before closing his fingertips around Cordero's nipple and giving it a rather nasty pinch.

Cordero flinched, but then he smiled at the stud, and he didn't do anything to discourage him when the fashion plate groped him even more brazenly—getting both of his hands into the act now, one on Cordero's pecs, the other on his crotch. Cordero submitted to the mauling, assuming it would lead to further intimacies.

"What a hot man," the clone groaned, and Cordero realized, to his dismay, that his sexy admirer was either drunk or stoned or both. Not that the man's attraction to Cordero seemed to be in any way feigned or exaggerated, but now that Cordero had had a chance to study him more closely, he could tell that the dude was impaired. "I'd like to take you home with me and let you do dirty things to me," he whispered into Cordero's ear, pressing his body firmly against Cordero's hard-muscled physique and feeling him up even more daringly than before, as though the two of them were alone in the barroom. "You can order me around and make me service you, like your submissive little bitch," the stranger offered. "Oh, I like it when a man gets rough with me."

Cordero's experience with anything which could be called *leather sex* or BDSM was extremely limited, and mostly confined to lurid fantasies about one man subduing and violating another. In these imaginings, Cordero was usually the submissive one. But he found the idea of being the aggressor almost as arousing.

Occasionally, when he masturbated, he'd buckle the dog collar tightly around his neck, apply the nipple clamps to his pecs, and lubricate either the dildo or the butt plug and use it to stimulate his anus. All the while, he'd pretend that some macho brute was *forcing* him to employ these toys.

Riley kept suggesting that he and Cordero should get into a full-blown *scene*, as he called it, but so far Cordero had always chickened out.

Ordinarily, having a guy promise to put himself at his mercy would have appealed to Cordero. But under the present circumstances, he was afraid if they did go home together, his intoxicated suitor would pass out on him, and Cordero would be venting his lust on his unconscious body. Cordero was as open-minded as any other gay guy, but he did draw the line at necrophilia!

"I'd let you do anything you wanted to me, sir." The hot-bodied little masochist insisted on using both hands to pull Cordero's nipples free from his tank top and stimulate them.

Cordero got off on the nipple play, and he was sorely tempted to take the guy up on his offer, to take advantage of his befuddled mental state and have his way with him. They could go to the guy's place, where Cordero could no doubt easily persuade him to lick his naked body all over, maybe even rim him, and then, in all probability, Cordero would fuck the shit out of his boyishly small, round ass.

And *then,* assuming the clone was still conscious at that point in the proceedings, Cordero could take his leave and go home to sleep in his own bed. Hit it and quit it! It would be raw, animalistic sex, pure physical release and nothing else.

Cordero could use a little of *that* as much as the next guy. But, for some reason, he was getting less and less interested in the prospect, despite his growing erection, which was creating an uncomfortable displacement inside the crotch of his jeans.

The clone's hands on his body, his obvious willingness, his sheer physical proximity, and Cordero's lusty imagination — they were all conspiring together to get Cordero hot. But his mind was oddly cold — almost turned off, in fact. *Damn!*

Cordero excused himself, and he went into the men's room to take a much-needed leak. All that beer he'd consumed was making his bladder beg to be emptied. His cock, when he extracted it from the fly of his jeans, was grossly swollen within the circle of the cock ring, and it seemed to take forever for it to relax enough to allow the urine to flow through it freely. *What a relief!* That was what Cordero thought, all he could think about, as he unloaded into the urinal. At that moment, pissing like that was almost as good as coming!

When he returned to the main room, he saw that his admirer was straddling a stool at the bar, drinking himself toward a stupor.

The man didn't even seem to notice Cordero's absence. Now realizing that he'd had a narrow escape, Cordero lingered at the far end of the bar, having another couple of beers and trading small talk with a couple of men with whom he had a casual acquaintance.

His night out was beginning to look like a failure.

Finally, Marc, the bartender cut Cordero's fickle admirer off and, despite his mumbled protests, called him a cab. When the cab arrived, the bar's thickset bouncer had to help the guy outside and dump him into the back seat of the vehicle.

Cordero decided he'd better call it a night, himself, before he ended up in a similar condition. It hadn't been a particularly memorable night out, but he was enough of a realist to cut his losses.

When he left the bar and headed home, he wasn't exactly drunk, but he was definitely feeling a buzz. His tank top was still disarranged from the clone's manipulation of his pecs, but the night air felt good on his torso and he didn't bother to adjust the shirt to cover up his nips.

Let anybody who wants to, go ahead and look. Cordero grinned to himself quite foolishly, as he observed the sparse late-night traffic on the streets. *Let them see that I'm built, that I'm hot. Not that it did me a hell of a lot of good tonight, though. Damn two-for-one night. Shit, I'm half drunk!*

He giggled. *Maybe some guy will come cruising along in his car and pick me up.*

As though by magic, his wish was granted, although not quite in the way he'd hoped!

When a police patrol car came up behind Cordero and slowed to a crawl beside him, he was feeling just silly enough to be titillated by the two police officers' casual scrutiny of him. Then, though, his instinctive wariness kicked in.

Oh, fuck! They're not going to arrest me, are they? Cordero returned the cops' gaze rather defiantly—which, of course, wasn't the smartest move on his part. *I'm not doing anything!* He supposed they could bust him for public intoxication, but that seemed like a stretch. He was hardly making a nuisance of himself. Admittedly, he was shambling along the sidewalk just a trifle unsteadily, but he was moving along, minding his own business.

"Hey, buddy," the cop closer to the curb called out, in a surprisingly pleasant tone of voice. He was young and blond, with medium-length hair and a neatly trimmed little mustache. He, like his partner, wasn't wearing his hat, so Cordero could get a good look at his face. He was handsome, and for some reason he looked oddly out of place in his starched and pressed blue uniform shirt—like a college jock or a preppy business executive who'd put on the cop uniform as a costume, just for one night. "Where're you headed?" he asked, as Cordero looked at him.

"Home," Cordero replied, still walking, although he slowed his pace to stay alongside the patrol car, which was crawling along in low gear.

"Straight home?"

"Straight home, to bed, to sleep," Cordero recited, dutifully.

"You been drinking?"

"A little, sure," Cordero admitted, more cautiously. He didn't want to risk spending the night locked up in a drunk tank. "But I'm not driving. I'm walking. I'm all right."

"Maybe. Do you have any ID on you?" As he spoke, the cop opened the patrol car's door and got out.

Grateful that he'd brought along his wallet after all, Cordero hauled it out and handed over his driver's license.

"All of twenty-two years old, are you, huh?"

"Ah—yes, sir."

"Think you know it all, don't you?"

"I'm not saying that," Cordero mumbled. "I'm not saying anything like that! I guess I'm old enough to drink, though."

"Maybe. But not to be a public nuisance."

"I'm not bothering anybody."

"There's such a thing as being a danger to yourself."

"I'm okay, officer, I swear!"

"Is this your current address, Mr. Tejera?"

"Yes, sir."

"I'm not crazy about the idea of you stumbling down the street in your condition. Hop in, and we'll give you a ride home."

"No, thanks, that's all right."

"Come on, we insist," the blond cop said, more coaxingly than anything else. "It's late, and we don't have anything better to do, and we want to keep you out of trouble. We'll see you home safe."

"Otherwise—if I refuse, if I don't play along—I guess you'll run me in?" Cordero asked, a bit sullenly.

"I hope it won't come to that. We're willing to give you a break. Work with us, okay?"

Cordero was beginning to get off on the whole scenario, so he got into the back seat of the patrol car. It had the usual barricade separating it from the front seat. The police officer's partner, a beefy beer-gutted number with florid cheeks, was doing the driving. He asked Cordero where he lived, and Cordero told him.

"We'll make the rounds of these side streets first, if you don't mind," the blond, who seemed to be the boss in the partnership, said.

"I'm in no hurry, officers." Cordero lounged in the back seat, languidly, as though he was royalty being chauffeured.

It did occur to him, though, that anybody who saw them drive past would assume he was under arrest, or at the very least a crime victim. But he was just intoxicated enough to find the thought vastly amusing.

A couple of cops, as my own personal drivers! I must be coming up in the world!

The cops drove through some of the darker, residential side streets, apparently at random, before returning to the main drag.

"Is this what you guys do all night?" Cordero asked. "Cruise around, looking for trouble?" It sounded a lot like typical gay activity to him!

"Looking for trouble, yeah," the blond cop replied, with a laugh. "And picking up strays like you."

"I'm a stray?"

"At the moment, yeah. Not unlike a tomcat, from the looks of you," he joked.

"Gee, thanks."

The cop continued to make small talk. "What bar did you go to tonight?"

Cordero told him the establishment's name.

"Isn't that a gay bar?" the beefy police officer behind the wheel blurted out.

His partner laughed again, more boisterously. "How would you know that?"

"By repute. And we get called to go there, occasionally. To break up fights, or roust drunks."

"That's true," the police officer agreed. "Although I must say, in general, the gay men in this town are well behaved."

"We pride ourselves on that," Cordero said, slyly.

The blond man emitted a faint snort. "What does your boyfriend think about you prowling around, this late at night?"

"What boyfriend?" Cordero retorted.

"Unattached, huh?"

"I'm so unattached, I'm constantly sliding off things," Cordero quipped. It wasn't the most brilliant witticism imaginable—in fact, it didn't make much sense, even to him—but after all, Cordero was buzzed, and definitely feeling no pain. He was also enjoying exchanging banter with the hot young cop, who intrigued him. The police officer didn't seem at all homophobic, for one thing. Quite the contrary. And he looked highly fuckable, for another!

He's no doubt straight. That was Cordero's conclusion, based, admittedly, on limited evidence. *What a waste!*

Imagine having a cop for a lover. The stud comes home, in that uniform, with all those accessories, including that gun strapped to his hip in its holster. Then he strips down naked. Doesn't even bother to shower, first, because he's so goddamn horny, so worked up after a long, stressful day on the job. No, the bastard just grabs you and throws you down on the bed and has his way with you! Making you suck on his cop dick. Shoving his cop cock up your ass! Fucking the shit out of you!

You lucky, cop-loving son of a bitch!

The fantasy made Cordero feel rather warm. He felt beads of sweat breaking out on his face and on his lightly clad torso and bare arms.

The two police officers stopped at a convenience store for coffee and donuts, and they insisted that Cordero share the goodies. So Cordero forced down a glazed donut and a paper cup of strong coffee during the short ride to his place.

"Is that helping to sober you up?" the fair-haired cop asked him.

"Yeah, a little," Cordero said. "Thanks."

Two cops taking a donut break — could anything be more stereotypical? Cordero was once again beginning to see some humor in the situation. He was in a good mood when the patrol car pulled up in front of his apartment building.

"You take care, now," the policeman said, as Cordero got out of the car.

"Sure. Thanks for the lift."

The cops waited, Cordero noticed, until he was safely inside the front door. He went upstairs, let himself into his apartment, and turned on the lights. Curious, he walked over to one of the windows overlooking the street, and he glanced out. Only then did he see the two cops drive off down the street, slowly, the red lights on top of their vehicle throwing an eerie glow through the lofty trees which pierced the sidewalks at intervals, and which obscured his view of parts of the neighboring buildings.

Cordero's encounter with the two representatives of law and order had a peculiar effect on his libido. Inexplicably, he was hornier than ever! He stumbled into the bathroom, where he took off all of his clothes, and he began to masturbate while standing in front of the sink. In the two bathroom mirrors, the one on the medicine cabinet door, and the full-length one on the adjacent wall, he stared lustfully at his naked body and metal-ringed cock under the bathroom's lighting fixtures.

He had a smear of donut glaze on his lip, but he didn't bother to wipe it off. He used one hand on his dick, and the other to tease his stiff and hotly responsive nipples, the way the clone had in the bar.

Wanting to see himself at full length while he jerked off, Cordero turned toward the bathroom's other mirror, the one on the wall. He posed in front of it, doing an imitation of a porn performer doing a solo scene for a video.

He thought about that blond cop, doing his best to picture the man naked. In Cordero's fantasy, the cop wasn't the genial number he'd been in the patrol car. On the contrary, he was tough and stern, even brutal. Feverishly, Cordero imagined him wrestling him to the ground, holding him down with his knee pressed into his back, while the cop wrenched his arms behind him and snapped a pair of handcuffs on his wrists. All the while, the gruff policeman warned him, in a tough snarl of a voice, not to resist.

"You're under arrest," Cordero imagined the cop telling him.

"I haven't done anything," Cordero whined.

"You're guilty of turning me on, you goddamn prickteaser," the

cop informed him. "Now you're going to have to take care of my hot, dirty cop dick!"

Abruptly, in one of those surreal shifts in continuity typical of dreams and sexual fantasies, the two men were in a jail cell. They were both nude and erect, and Cordero's hands were still cuffed behind his back. Belly-down on the bunk, he was being fucked up the ass by that sexy bastard's cock, which felt huge as it stretched and filled his cringing anus, really reaming out his hole!

"Confess, you lousy, stinking perp," the stud cop kept shouting at him, the whole time he screwed Cordero with such ruthless, unrelenting energy. "Confess, goddamn you, or I'll tear your hole wide open!"

"I confess, officer," Cordero imagined himself responding. "I confess that I'm a cocksucker — that I'm a dirty pervert — that I like to take a cock up my ass!"

"But you especially like cop dick, don't you, boy?" the cop taunted him. "You like that, best of all, huh? Admit it!"

"Yeah — yeah, I like cop dick," Cordero heard himself babbling. "Can't get enough of it, officer!"

"That's better," the cop grunted. "Now, you're going to give me the name of every goddamn queer you've ever been with. So I can bust them, too. Haul their asses in here and fuck every single one of them — !"

That would be quite a long list of names, and screwing all those guys would keep Cordero's fantasy cop so busy that he'd need to put in a hell of a lot of overtime! But logic and reality never played much of a part, when a horny gay guy was allowing lewd images to flash through his overheated brain while he was jacking off. The important consideration was that the thought of being worked over by that hot cop was definitely doing it for Cordero. He was ready to pop!

"Dirty cop! You're probably on the take. Bastard — cop bastard! Hurt me, uh, yeah, hurt me, you son of a bitch! Beat me. I like it, I want it. Stinking cop!"

Weirdly, contempt for the handsome officer of the law only

seemed to drive a spur into Cordero's lust, maddening him, pushing him over the edge into orgasm. He pictured himself as the object of cruel police brutality, and the sadomasochistic mental images, as vague and dreamlike as they were, tapped his flow of hot, impetuous sperm, which rushed through him.

"Motherfucking goddamn stud cop!" Cordero yelped, aloud, his voice echoing off the bathroom walls. "Cop dick! Yeah, you son of a bitch, give me that cop dick! Aw, shit—"

He came quickly, the pressure of the cock ring making his cockshaft pulse more forcibly than usual when it spat out its thick white wads of sexual venom, which spattered all over the polished glass of the mirror above the sink. Not even bothering to clean himself up, Cordero staggered into the bedroom. The last thing he remembered was his flushed, almost feverish face hitting the cool pillow on his bed. Then he was out—blissfully unconscious.

In the morning, the entire episode had faded to a dreamlike unreality in Cordero's memory—except for the physical evidence, consisting of the cock ring he was still wearing, his cruising outfit discarded in a heap on the bathroom floor, and the dried semen stains on the bathroom mirror and the porcelain of the sink.

Cordero thought about those television crime shows, in which the detectives used a special ultraviolet light to detect body fluids at a crime scene. If they used that device in his place, his whole bathroom would light up, providing unmistakable, irrefutable evidence of his guilt!

Cordero smirked.

Well, there isn't any law about jerking off and spilling your cum all over the place. Or about consensual sex between adults, including same-sex sucking and fucking, for that matter! That hot cop can't bust me for that. I almost wish he would, though. I'd like that sexy bastard to snap his cuffs on me and take me into custody. And then, work me over. Beat the shit out of me, and fuck me! Fuck me, hard!

"I want to plead guilty, officer," Cordero mumbled to himself, aloud. "I'm guilty as hell—of being horny, of jerking off—of shooting my load! Go ahead and arrest me. If you're man enough!"

CHAPTER THREE: DREAM MASTER

Cordero lay in his bed one night. He felt restless, unable to fall asleep right away, and he had sprung a hard-on which, although he tried to ignore it, stubbornly refused to go down. His boner was like a tent pole, holding up the sheet which was all that was covering Cordero's body on this warm night. His penis was making increasingly urgent demands for immediate manual attention, twitching like a divining rod pointing the way to underground water, except that it was aiming upward, toward the ceiling. The fucking thing throbbed like mad between Cordero's belly and the sheet he'd pulled up to his chest.

Damn! I've got a real hard cock! Big goddamn boner. Real stiff! Shit, I wish I could make the motherfucker go down, go soft, and let me alone — leave me in peace, and let me get to sleep. No such luck, though, from the feel of it! Hard — fuck, yeah, I'm rock hard!

I could always go ahead and jerk off, I guess. But no — that's kid stuff. Might as well save this hard-on, save my load, for some lucky guy.

If I can hold out that long!

With a real effort of willpower, Cordero forced himself to ignore his nagging tumescence.

After a few moments, he could feel himself dozing off.

As was often the case when he was dreaming, the locale in which the scenario was being played out was vague. It was an interior, but Cordero could discern few details. He couldn't even decide whether it was day or night.

There was no doubt about the identities of the two participants, though. Cordero was one of them. That handsome,
young, blond cop was the other.

And their roles were well-defined. Cordero was the submissive. The cop was the dominant.

*"Fuck me," Cordero begged, like the cheap, shameless man whore
he was.*

The police officer sneered at him.

*"I don't think so." He growled the words. "Not yet, anyway! You
don't deserve it, punk. You want this big, fat, hard cop dick of
mine?" As he spoke, he hefted his genitals in the palm of his hand,
holding them out toward Cordero, like an offering, although one
which was tantalizingly just outside of his reach.*

*Cordero licked his slavering lips with his tongue. His mouth was
watering at the sight of the other man's massive uncut phallus!
Sheathed in foreskin, the glans looked enormous, but it was mounted
upon an equally impressive shaft — long, thick, and, at the moment,
absolutely inflexible. Already, in his imagination, Cordero could feel
that rigid penis inside his mouth, filling him, stretching his jaws
apart, jabbing toward the back of his mouth, and sliding down into
his throat with choking force.*

*"Yeah — I want it — I want it in my mouth, up my ass!" he whim-
pered. "You know I do!"*

*"Too bad," the cop told him, contemptuously. "You want this
meat? You have to earn it. What're you willing to do, to earn that
privilege?"*

"Anything," Cordero vowed.

*"Then you can start by showing me some proper respect." Lean-
ing over Cordero, the cop slapped his face — hard! Cordero recoiled
from the stinging blow. "Bitch, when you open your mouth and talk
to me, you'd better address me with the proper respect! I want to
hear you call me officer or sir at all times." To drive home the message, the police officer delivered another slap. "Are you ready to
show some respect for the law, punk?"*

"Yes, sir." Cordero hastened to assure his tormentor he could

show the proper respect.

"*Then get that mouth and tongue of yours going on me, you dirty cocksucker! I want to feel you lick and suck every part of my body. Worship these cop muscles of mine. Give me a nice wet tongue bath. Pay special attention to my armpits and my crotch and my ass. They feel kind of hot and sweaty and funky. Swab them, bitch! Clean them off.*"

Cordero obeyed, with alacrity.

In his vivid, detailed dream, they were both naked. Cordero was on his knees in front of the brutish cop, with his wrists handcuffed behind his back. Even out of uniform, the cop was an imposing physical presence, a cruel taskmaster, whom Cordero defied at his peril. Cordero was his prisoner — helpless to resist, no matter how degrading or disgusting the demands the policeman might make of him, as his sadistic whims inspired him.

In his dream, Cordero wasn't new to the role of the good-looking cop's bitch. No, he imagined that the two of them had a long-term, ongoing relationship. And one based on sex! This was just a game, involving roleplaying, which they'd indulged in often because they both enjoyed it. Cordero had learned to love it. Only a short time previously, he'd never imagined that he would have a police officer as a fuck buddy, let alone that he'd agree to be his submissive little bitch when they had sex.

"*Come on, you can do better than that, and we both damn well know it,*" the stern cop taunted Cordero, while Cordero swabbed his damp, sweaty armpits with his tongue, tasting the salty residue of the man's hot perspiration on his flesh. "*Lick and suck those stinking cop pits, boy! Keep that tongue of yours moving, all over them. And sniff — sniff them! Inhale that frigging pit aroma. You know it always gets you good and high.*"

"*Yes, sir,*" Cordero moaned as he worked on him.

The cop had his nightstick in his hand. He reached down and tapped the baton against Cordero's bare buttocks.

"I ought to shove this baton up your ass," he threatened Cordero. "That should loosen up that hole of yours. Then you'll be able to take my dick."

"Put it in me, sir," Cordero invited him.

The cop grimaced, his handsome features distorted by lust into a satyr-like mask.

"No, you'd enjoy that too much. God, you're disgusting," he spat at Cordero. "I don't know why I waste my time on you." Still holding the baton in one fist, he lightly, teasingly, tapped Cordero's ass cheeks with it. He used his other hand to grab a fistful of Cordero's sweaty, disheveled hair. "Now my stinking crotch," he commanded, forcing Cordero's face down to his groin. "Scrub it with your tongue! And, when you've got that squeaky clean, then you're going to stick your tongue in my ass and clean out my hole. Who needs toilet paper when you've got a cop-loving sex slave to take care of you? You do a good job of that, boy, and maybe – just maybe – I'll let you suck my dick, and I'll shove it up your ass!"

"Yes, sir," Cordero babbled, groveling before him. "Whatever you say, officer!"

"Cop whore," the stud taunted Cordero. "You're nothing but a dirty little cop whore, aren't you, boy?"

"That's right, sir," Cordero told him.

God help me – I am a cop whore! Even as the realization flashed through his mind, though, Cordero had to admit something else, which was even more shameful.

And the worst part of it is – I'm proud of it—

Something jarred him awake. After a moment's confusion and disorientation, he realized that he was in his apartment, in his bedroom, in his bed – late at night, warm and comfortable under the covers, with the light off. Disappointment surged through him when he understood that the hot cop of his dream had been no more than a fantasy figure, now gone.

Aw, shit! The whole thing was just a dream. A filthy, nasty, disgusting sex dream!

That cop — good-looking, arrogant bastard! Well, he's good for one thing. To jack off over!

I shouldn't jerk off — but why not? What the fuck!

Giving in to his urgent, lustful need, at last, Cordero flipped the sheet aside, baring his groin. He reached down, took his cock in his hand, and stroked it, absentmindedly, into full and demanding erection, while he thought about the man in uniform. He tried to imagine what the police officer would look like naked, and how large his cock would be when it, like Cordero's, was wholly engorged. Cordero examined the smooth surface of his fuck tool with his fingertips, rubbing its shaft lightly, using the sweating flat of his palm to massage and tease himself. It felt good to play with himself like that.

He was leading such a promiscuous sex life lately, that he rarely had to resort to masturbation to relieve himself. Now, though, he lost himself in his self-pleasuring.

He manipulated himself, roughly, unsparingly, playing with his always responsive cock. His penis never failed him. It was ever ready to enjoy some fun at night before its owner drifted off to sleep.

In a matter of minutes, Cordero had worked up his cock to its full rigidity, and he had begun a slow but effective hydraulic pumping of the looser flesh surrounding the hard core of his shaft. He visualized the police officer again, pretending that it was he who was giving him the hand job. What a looker that stud was! How hot he'd probably be in bed, if only he liked guys!

Fucker, you big-dicked fucker! With all those muscles bulging inside your uniform, making the seams look like they're about to burst. I bet you pack a long, thick nightstick in those tight pants. Yeah, I know that fat, hard cop cock of yours would feel good in my mouth — down my throat — up my ass! Bet you aren't circumcised, are you, officer? Fat, meaty uncut prick — probably has a nice flap of foreskin, for me to get my tongue inside! Yeah, man, give me a chance to get you in bed with me, just once. I'll show you such a good time that you'll turn gay. You'll start coming back to me for more! Begging me for sex!

You won't be calling me boy and punk and bitch then, tough guy. Hell, no. You'll be the one down on your knees. You'll be my goddamn cop sex slave!

Cordero's climax came sluggishly, but very intensely, his sperm erupting like thick hot white lava over the flat, hard muscles of his torso, wetting him down, dripping in slimy rivulets down the creases of his solidly-muscled body. Cordero grunted with satisfaction as he squeezed his dick dry with his fist, and then he wiped himself off with the towel which he always kept handy in the nightstand next to his bed, in anticipation of just such cleanups.

The apartment wasn't air conditioned. It was well-supplied, though, with vintage ceiling fans, old enough to qualify as antiques. One of these rotated high above Cordero's head as he lay, and it circulated the air. Through the screens in the open bedroom windows, he could hear muted traffic noises, coming up from the street below.

A guy. That was what Cordero thought, drowsily, only half-coherently. *All I need is a guy, here in bed with me. Sleeping with me. Ready, though, to suck and fuck, any time I happen to wake up, in the middle of the night, or in the morning. A guy – yeah, some hot guy. Some stud! Like that sexy prickteaser, that cop. The bitch! The hot goddamn straight bitch!*

What a waste, him being straight. If only!

He drew the sheet back over himself, and, relaxing on the bed which was warmed by his naked body, he stopped thinking about the provocative police officer or indeed about anything else, as he sank quickly into a dreamless and restorative sleep.

CHAPTER FOUR: AN UNEXPECTED VISITOR

Two nights later, Cordero was at home alone. It was another warm night, and, as he often did in the privacy of his apartment, he wore only a pair of boxer shorts.

It was Friday night, but he had no intention of going out. The bars would be crowded and noisy, the competition intense. And his abortive encounter with the drunken clone had soured him on the whole idea of cruising, for a while.

I'll stay home, for a change. Make an early night of it, and get some shuteye.

When the doorbell rang, it startled Cordero, because he wasn't expecting anybody.

Wonder who that could be? One of the guys from school, maybe?

For the hundredth time, he reminded himself that his next apartment would need to have the amenity of an intercom system. He found his keys and clutched them in his hand, so he wouldn't risk locking himself out. Leaving the door ajar, he went downstairs, barefoot. The tenants had a small vestibule, with their mailboxes along one wall, each one with a doorbell button under it. To gain access beyond the vestibule, they had to pass through a security door, which had a keypad lock on the outside and a crash bar inside. Using the bar to open the security door, while he looked through its glass window, Cordero was even more startled to find none other than the blond cop standing there in the vestibule — crisp blue uniform and all!

Without thinking, Cordero opened the door.

For the first time, now that they were face to face in a good light, Cordero saw the name machine-stitched on the right-hand chest of the cop's blue uniform shirt—*Kovary*. That was an Eastern European surname if Cordero had ever heard one, and the handsome stud certainly looked the part.

"Hi," the young policeman said when he caught sight of Cordero's half-naked body in the now open doorway. "I happened to be passing by, and I saw your lights on, and I wondered if you were home." He paused. Evidently, he was waiting for a response. But Cordero was too astonished to say anything at first.

Then Cordero asked, "My lights? How'd you know which apartment is mine?"

"Saw you turn them on, before we drove off the other night. In my job it pays to be observant. So it wouldn't have been hard, just now, to figure out which doorbell must be yours, even if I didn't remember your name from your driver's license. Aren't you going to invite me in, Mr. Tejera?"

"Aren't you on duty?"

"I just got off. I'm working some strange hours this week. Filling in for guys who are on vacation or sick leave, that sort of shit."

"I see. Is this an official visit, or is it a social call?"

The cop grinned. "Social—assuming you're feeling sociable tonight. Official only if you think we have any unfinished business to take care of. Or—were you planning to go out later on?" he asked, with just a hint of archness and mockery in his tone of voice. "If you are, I hope you're planning to put some more clothes on first."

"Oh, yeah, that's right," Cordero said, matching his unexpected visitor's manner. "I'd forgotten that it was your job to keep me out of trouble. Well—as long as you're here, you'd better come on upstairs."

While he led the way to his apartment, Cordero was suddenly self-conscious about his near-nudity. Following him up the stairs, the cop could no doubt see Cordero's bare back, the play of muscles in his thighs and calves, and the rippling movement of his buttocks inside the seat of the baggy boxer shorts. Some instinct told Cordero that the cop *was* looking at all these things. After all, he'd just boasted about being observant!

"I see you survived your little adventure the other night," Officer Kovary observed when they were in Cordero's living room.

"Thanks to you. Not that I mind you taking such a personal interest in me, but who appointed you to be my guardian angel in blue, anyway?"

"I appointed myself." The cop reached out and touched Cordero's bare chest—lightly, pressing his fingertips against one firm pectoral muscle, not even rubbing or stroking the flesh, but simply touching.

Cordero was nervous, but he didn't step backward or do anything else to pull away from the other man, or to discourage him.

"Nice pecs," Kovary murmured. "You don't mind me touching you like this, do you?"

"It's okay," Cordero replied, trying to project a casualness when he was, in fact, feeling anything but casual.

"Then maybe you won't mind this, either."

Leaning forward, Kovary kissed Cordero on the lips, a gentle peck, not explicitly sexual, but a contact which made a tingle of hot arousal surge through him. That sexy little mustache on the police officer's upper lip tickled Cordero's own lips.

Well, that pretty much decides that! Jesus, this cop is gay, all right! And he thinks I'm gay, too! And not just gay—available. Kind of bold of him, taking that for granted—assuming I'm willing to fool around with him.

Not that he's wrong!

"Ah—maybe we'd better take it slow," Cordero cautioned the other man.

"What's the matter? Don't you like me?"

"I like you just fine. But I don't really know you. Let's at least sit down and have a drink, before we, uh—move on to anything else."

"Fine," Officer Kovary said, amiably enough.

"Beer?"

"That'd be great."

Cordero went into the kitchen, where he fetched two bottles of beer from his refrigerator. Soon he and the cop were seated in the living room, relaxing, drinking. Cordero felt a bit uncomfortable, nearly nude while his guest was fully dressed.

"Maybe I'd better go put some clothes on," Cordero suggested.

"Don't bother on my account. What do you think I do, the minute I get home after work? I lose the uniform."

An image of the policeman stripping naked, and what he might look like when he was nude, flashed through Cordero's mind. "If you don't mind my saying so—" Cordero began to say, falteringly, in an attempt to keep the conversation going.

"Yes?"

"Kind of ballsy, isn't it, coming here uninvited?"

The cop shrugged—and smiled. He seemed immune to self-consciousness. "You can always throw me out on my ass."

"Not sure I'd care to try to manhandle a police officer."

"Not even if he might like being manhandled?"

Hearing that, Cordero continued to wonder whether this was real, or just some fantasy being played out inside his head. *Is he really coming on to me? And if he's not, then what the hell is he here for? What does he want from me?*

"Well, as long as you're here, you're welcome to stay."

"Thanks. I must say, this is pleasant. But we need to get one thing clear from the get-go," the cop said.

"Yeah? What's that?" Cordero asked.

"I'm not interested in a relationship. I like to play the field. All I'm interested in is sex."

You, and most of the other men in this town!

"And you're telling me this because . . ."

"Just don't want you to get your hopes up."

"Have a high opinion of yourself, do you, officer?"

"I flatter myself I'm not exactly repulsive."

"You're assuming, of course, I want to have sex with you."

"Don't you?"

"Maybe. I do like to have some say in the matter, though. Not be taken for granted. I told you, the other night, I was at that gay bar. So, you naturally assume I'm easy. Willing to go to bed with just any guy who comes along. Is that it?"

"Aren't you? Willing to do just that, I mean?"

"Oh, nice," Cordero fumed.

"I may have ambitions of becoming a detective, some day," Kovary said, slyly. "Which means I'm trying to get into the habit of deducing things, from the evidence. I put one and one together. That makes two, usually."

"Usually, maybe. Not always, dude. Maybe I'm choosy. About whom I fuck around with." Cordero spoke boldly — defiantly.

But Kovary seemed unperturbed. There was that bland self-assurance about the man which Cordero found rather annoying, indeed rather infuriating. He was a cocky bastard. Smug. Cordero hated his guts! "Consensual sex, of course," Kovary murmured. He now seemed, to Cordero, to be presenting himself as the epitome and the voice of reason. "What else? What's wrong? *Do* you find me repulsive? I'm not your type?"

"You're okay," Cordero conceded. "Maybe a little full of yourself."

"I imagine you're right. Sorry about that."

"Don't be nice," Cordero advised.

"Why not? Why shouldn't I?"

"It doesn't suit you. I admit it—I like you better when you're in your prick mode. *Officer,*" Cordero spat out, as an afterthought, with ironic, mock respect.

The policeman guffawed, suddenly in the grip of quite spontaneous-sounding laughter. "You're all right, my friend," he declared. "I like you. And—you're not quite as much of a pushover as I thought you were, when we first met." He was scrutinizing Cordero intently, appraisingly, in a way which made Cordero feel not just half-naked, but totally nude, exposed and vulnerable. "I like a guy with spirit. With balls. And you. You're a very bad boy, aren't you?" the cop asked.

"Huh? What do you mean?"

"Whoring around," the police officer responded bluntly. "Going out, late at night. Getting drunk in gay bars. Trying to pick up men, for sex."

"I'm old enough to drink, I'm old enough to be in bars, and as you yourself said a moment ago, there's such a thing as consensual sex between adults, which isn't against the law," Cordero blustered.

Kovary smiled. "You talk like a typical jailhouse lawyer. You know, one of those guys who always thinks he knows his rights."

"I guess I know some of them."

"When I saw you walking down the street the other night," Kovary remarked, "I thought to myself, *Oh, God, I bet he's making the rounds of all the bars. I can't believe he hasn't gotten himself picked up yet!* You looked so hot."

"Thanks. But I struck out, in that one bar I went to. Sometimes you get lucky—and other times, you don't."

Kovary nodded. "Yeah, I know just what you're talking about."

31

"Aw, come on. A guy as good-looking as you? You must not have any problems getting laid."

"Some men are *very* choosy, and they're only attracted to a specific type. Which is their right. But I think it's a shame, in a way. They're limiting their possibilities. I like all kinds of guys. A man doesn't have to be drop-dead handsome, or have a great body, to be sexy." Kovary smiled at Cordero. "That wasn't a reference to you, buddy. You're easy on the eyes, and that may not be a requirement, but it never hurts."

Cordero was intrigued by the fact that the other man was so open about his homosexuality—with him, anyway. "What's it like, being a gay cop?" he asked.

The cop shrugged. "Probably not all that different from being gay in any other line of work."

"Still—I don't think of the typical policeman as being all that open-minded, or enlightened."

"That's true."

"Are you out on your job?" Cordero inquired.

"Yes, and no. Not officially. But once I get to know one of the other guys well—then I may confide in him. Usually, it turns out to be no big deal. And occasionally, it results in something happening outside of work."

"You mean—cops fooling around with each other?"

"It happens. Huh, the thought gets you excited, does it? I can tell by the look on your face."

"Wow, that *is* exciting. Like a porn fantasy come to life."

Kovary grunted. "It's okay, except when one of the guys wants to play cop in the bedroom. I don't mean in a role-playing way—that can be hot. I mean, thinking he has to keep up the kind of tough-guy act that's useful on the job. I have my fuck buddies on the force. Civilians, too. But recently I seem to be going through a dry spell. It's been a while since I've met anybody—interesting," Kovary murmured, in a faltering kind of way, looking and sounding unsure of himself for the first time since he and Cordero had met.

Cordero smiled. "Am I interesting?"

"Interesting, yeah—and exciting. Looking at you, I'm getting all stirred up right now, as a matter of fact," the cop whispered. "Want to do me a favor, buddy?"

"What?"

"Lose the shorts," the cop pleaded, again in a whisper. "Drop the fucking underwear. Let me see you naked."

"Okay. Why not?" Cordero replied, all detachment on the outside, although internally he could feel himself in the grip of a growing excitement, which was accelerating his breathing and his pulse rate.

What was he getting himself into? Sex, obviously. Sex with a cop! An exciting prospect, to be sure. But sex—a familiar enough activity—nonetheless. Still, there seemed to be more to it than that. Kovary projected a hint of potential danger, of strong emotions simmering below the surface, which gave Cordero an extra frisson of excitement—excitement, mixed with wariness, if not actual fear.

Cordero took a final swig of beer, and then he set the empty bottle down on the coffee table. Standing up, he dropped his boxers down around his ankles. Freeing his feet from the shorts, he kicked them aside.

"Yeah, you've got a real nice body," Kovary whispered, ogling Cordero. His stare had an intensity which Cordero found rather off-putting. There was lust in the look, but also an undercurrent of something deeper, almost sinister.

"Okay, now I'm starting to feel a little self-conscious," Cordero told his guest—playfully, although there was an undercurrent of anxiety in his voice and manner. "With me being nude, and you still dressed—in that uniform, no less. Why don't you get comfortable?"

"Sure," the police officer agreed. "If you'll turn around for a minute, and not look."

"Don't tell me you're shy?" Cordero protested.

"No, I just don't want you to watch while I find someplace to hide my gun."

"Hide it? Why? Do you think I'm going to use it on you?"

"I'd like to see you try." As Kovary spoke, Cordero noticed that the cop's stern facial expression relaxed a bit. Was he actually permitting himself to crack just a hint of a smile? "But don't be offended. It's a force of habit. A precaution. When I go home, the first thing I do it take off my gun and secure it."

"All right. I'll close my eyes and count to ten, twenty, whatever. Tell me when you're done."

Whatever Kovary did, he was stealthy about it. Cordero didn't hear a thing—not even his footsteps on the floor. Counting slowly inside his head, Cordero had reached *nine* when the policeman said, "Okay, now you can look."

He turned around and opened his eyes.

The cop was standing there with his holster empty, the handgun nowhere to be seen. Unbuckling his utility belt, he took it off. He began to unbutton his blue uniform shirt, first the cuffs, and then down the front. Shrugging off the shirt, he revealed the tank-top style white undershirt he worn under it. The snug-fitting garment hugged his muscular torso, baring his shoulders and arms, and displaying his pecs to good advantage. The view was even better after he pulled the undershirt up, over his head, and off, discarding it as well and then standing there stripped to the waist.

Cordero was looking at him intently—which, Cordero realized, probably hadn't escaped his notice. It was rude to stare, but some things were well worth staring at.

"Like what you see?" Kovary inquired.

"No complaints so far," Cordero told him. "Keep going, though."

The striptease continued. The cop sat down to remove his

shoes and socks. He stood up again to drop his trousers. Finally, he was down to his briefs, which matched the undershirt. After a moment of what struck Cordero as incongruously coy hesitation, he shed the briefs, as well. Now he and Cordero were both nude.

When Cordero stepped forward to embrace his enigmatic guest again, he hesitated. Admiring the man's hard, obviously weight-trained physique, Cordero discovered that this cop was kinkier than he'd suspected. The man was wearing an improvised cock ring which lifted his cock and balls up and out, at a high angle. From the superficial glimpse he got of it, Cordero guessed that it was no ordinary genital restraint.

"Anything wrong?" Kovary asked.

"Not at all."

"Come on, then. Don't just stand there looking at me. It's okay to touch, too."

Cordero took the cop in his arms. The man's cock and balls were hoisted so high that they pressed against Cordero's abdomen when he kissed the guy again, their chests touching, their hands resting on each other's backs.

With his tongue in the cop's mouth, Cordero reached down between their bodies to fondle his prick and examine the genital restraint. He saw that the cop had taken a long piece of some sort of small-gauge electrical wire, coated with plastic, and he'd wound it around his cock and balls several times. Then he'd looped the wire around his testicles in an X pattern to keep them separated from the shaft of his dick.

The wire was still wound tightly enough to retain the shape into which it was molded around the genitals, but the soft plastic coating insulated it, so it wouldn't chafe. Kind of ingenious and practical, in fact, Cordero thought. The cop hadn't knotted it. The two ends were simply twisted tightly together between his thighs. Cordero could feel the copper ends of the wire sticking out where they had been cut.

"Unusual cock ring," Cordero murmured.

"I like the way it feels," the cop responded, almost shyly. "I had part of the spool of that wire left over from a home improvement project. Thought I'd put it to good use. It's adjustable—flexible. And disposable. Plus, you can use it just like rope, to tie up somebody. Twist the ends tight enough and he can't get loose." Then the man smiled, looking more confident. "Of course, most of the time, the guy doesn't want to get free."

"Interesting," Cordero murmured.

"You like cock rings, do you?"

"Yes."

"Have you got one, too? That you can put on?"

"Yeah."

"Will you put it on for me?"

"If you want. Come on."

CHAPTER FIVE: SUBMITTING TO AU-THORITY

Cordero decided that it was time to adjourn to the bedroom. Before he led the other guy there, though, he gave in to a sudden, rash impulse. He grabbed the man's hand. To his relief, Kovary didn't pull away but returned the manual pressure. It was odd, a strange sort of intimacy, feeling the cop's slightly moist, warm palm clasped against his own. *I'm holding his hand. The cop's hand. So weird. As though he was intimate with me – maybe my boyfriend, my lover!*

Cordero didn't turn on the bedroom lamp. Enough light penetrated from the other room through the door, which he left open, to cast an appropriately intimate pattern of light and shadow over the bed.

He opened a drawer in his bureau, found his stainless steel cock ring, and slipped it on, deliberately aiming his dick at the policeman while he did so, making a display of the process.

"Nice," the cop said, staring at Cordero's groin, sounding breathless.

The police officer reached out with both hands, touched Cordero's bare shoulders, and then he slid his fingertips lightly down Cordero's arms, again just grazing the flesh. His palms moved to cup Cordero's pecs, and then he closed his fingers around his twin mounds of chest muscle, compressing them hard.

He pinched both of Cordero nipples, and the recipient of the rough treatment gasped when the pressure on his pecs sent a corresponding hot throb of response through his cock, which strained against the metal circle surrounding its base.

The cop pinched his nipples harder, almost sadistically, and Cordero grunted, involuntarily, his knees buckling. Still gripping the pecs between his thumbs and fingertips, the cop tugged on them, pulling Cordero's chest against his own, and he kissed Cordero on the mouth, pushing his way between his lips with his tongue and licking the edges of his teeth.

Cordero stood there kissing the cop and letting him work on his nips for several breathless minutes until it felt as though his pecs were on fire.

Feeling more bold, Cordero reached up and grasped the cop's head, raking his fingers through his hair, and he kissed him harder, increasing the pressure of their lips and forcing his own tongue deep inside the other man's mouth. The cop tasted of mint mouthwash, the flavor intense and stinging on Cordero's tongue. Cordero speculated whether that was for his benefit. A swig of mouthwash that morning, before the police officer had left his home to report to work, couldn't have lasted so long. He must have kept a second bottle in his locker at the police station, and he'd refreshed the interior of his mouth before he clocked out at the end of his shift. He hadn't swung by Cordero's place impulsively, on the spur of the moment. No, he'd hoped Cordero would be home. He'd anticipated kissing Cordero, sooner or later!

As they kissed and Cordero's nipples pulsated within the cop's grip, Cordero groaned with pleasure. He ground his crotch against his visitor's, letting his swollen, ringed prick rub firmly against the matching protuberance of the cop's erection, which was equipped with its own peculiar, home-made genital harness.

Both men were gasping for breath by the time the cop broke their kiss, and, releasing Cordero's pecs, he took a step back. He helped himself to Cordero's cock and balls, massaging restlessly over the head and shaft of his rigid penis and his bloated testicles, and twisting his cock ring around and around as if turning a socket wrench or a screwdriver.

Cordero was going crazy with desire and frustration. He couldn't decide which was more arousing — the sight of this naked stud standing in front of him, sporting his own huge, hard erection — or the way his own body responded, instinctively, helplessly, to the other man's touch.

He moaned with sheer physical relief when the cop suddenly let go of him, dropped down to the floor on his knees, and stuffed Cordero's dick inside his mouth.

The young policeman sucked Cordero ravenously, bobbing his head back and forth in his crotch, uttering obscene slurping sounds, his lips caressing the circumference of Cordero's shaft and literally kissing his cock ring, which nestled under his mustache and tapped audibly against his teeth a couple of times.

In mid-suck, Cordero retaliated for the stimulation the cop had provided his nips with some pec play of his own. Instinctively recognizing his new sex partner's need, Cordero crouched over him, reached down, and seized his big, brown nipples, pinching them, pulling them away from his pectoral muscles, digging his fingernails into the turgid cones of flesh, and twisting them.

The cop took all of this abuse, like a man, without complaint or struggle. If anything, he burrowed his face into Cordero's groin more tightly and he sucked his cock more avidly — using his hands, now, to fondle Cordero's buttocks and tickle his balls.

The sex play turned into a nude wrestling match, the combatants grappling together, each striving for the physical advantage in a struggle for dominance.

The two men ended up, to Cordero's bemusement, on the

floor of Cordero's bedroom, sixty-nining like mad.

What the fuck? This is ridiculous! There's a perfectly good bed going to waste right there beside us. But I'm so hot for this guy. I don't care about that. I'm willing to put up with a little discomfort, for the time being.

The cop demonstrated a ravenous hunger for Cordero's cock. Cordero had rarely been sucked so well, or so enthusiastically. The guy's mouth was like a vacuum cleaner, exerting its strong suction on his fuck tool!

He interrupted his chowing down on Cordero's dick, in fact, only once. Gasping for breath, he begged Cordero, "Bite my cock. Use your teeth on it. I'm into a little pain. Come on, don't worry, I can take it. Grab hold of my fucking foreskin between your teeth and yank on it. Then chew on my frigging cockhead! Do it, fucker. Leave your teeth marks on me!"

He was kind of kinky, obviously. Cordero did his best to comply with his demands.

After a few more minutes of biting and nibbling and sucking, on Cordero's part, and of comparatively straightforward fellatio on the cop's part, of which the latter was undeniably sheer bliss for Cordero, the police officer released his dick and he rose to his feet, smiling at Cordero.

"You're one hell of a hot man," he complimented Cordero.

"Right back at you. Come on," Cordero pleaded. "Let's lie down."

They climbed onto the bed. They made out. Despite his obvious eagerness, now the cop didn't attack Cordero in the aggressive way he'd anticipated, as some of his pickups did. Instead, the man seemed as interested in touching and kissing as in actual genital stimulation.

Not that there wasn't plenty of that! When he wasn't sucking on his nipples or using his hands on them, the cop seemed to be sucking on Cordero's cock. Cordero did his best to keep up with him. Cordero didn't know what kinds of sausages were popular in Eastern Europe or featured in the traditional cuisine of Americans of that ancestry. But this fucker's phallus was one hell of a meaty, spicy mouthful! Once Cordero had enjoyed a taste of it, he couldn't get enough of it!

After their second excruciatingly intense and enjoyable bout of sixty-nining, though, the two men broke away from each other, and Kovary gasped, "Do you like to fuck?"

"Sure."

"Do you want to fuck *me?*"

Cordero couldn't believe he'd heard correctly. "Yeah, if you want me to."

"You bet I want you to. I really need it, tonight."

Kovary was so goddamn macho that Cordero was surprised to hear that he took it up the ass. But that didn't deter him! The mere thought of penetrating and possessing the other man's hot stud cop butt got Cordero so excited that he was afraid his treacherous dick might spurt out its fuck fluid, spontaneously, without any need of direct stimulation.

"But first—wait." Kovary got off the bed, and he sauntered back into the living room, returning a moment later with his discarded uniform trousers in his hand. Through the unusually wide belt loops, his black leather utility belt was threaded. He unsnapped his handcuffs from the belt. "First I'm going to put these on you."

Cordero was dumbfounded. "Why?"

"Because we both know you want me to."

"I thought you wanted me to fuck you."

"I do."

"How am I supposed to do that, with those on?"

"I'll show you. Turn around. Hands behind your back. I'm sure you know the drill."

"If you're implying I've ever been arrested—I haven't."

Kovary grinned. "I was thinking about all the cop shows you've no doubt seen."

"Oh."

"Now, relax."

Cordero felt the cold steel hoops of the cuffs being closed around his wrists, keeping them restrained behind him, in the small of his back, just above his butt. Experimentally, he wriggled his fingers, and he tried to tug his arms apart—in vain, of course. His arm muscles bulged as he strained against the handcuffs, feeling the steel press into the flesh of his wrists.

"Shit," he moaned.

"Relax," Kovary repeated. "You look good, cuffed like that."

Cordero was aware of an odd, subtle change in the cop. He seemed quite relaxed, himself, with only his erection betraying his sexual excitement. There was a soft, silky, insinuating tone in his voice.

His warm hands moved to Cordero's behind, gripping, kneading, and massaging them.

"Nice ass," Kovary purred. "It's taking me all my will-power to keep myself from fucking it. But a promise is a promise. You can still have mine—this time. Where do you keep your lube? There next to the bed?"

"Yeah," Cordero replied.

"You mean *yes, sir*, don't you?"

"Sorry. Yes, sir."

"Well, maybe I'll overlook it this time, and not insist on too much formality. After all, we're about to become quite intimately acquainted." Again, there was that caressing timbre in the cop's voice. Cordero shivered. There was something more sinister about the way Kovary was speaking to him than any barked verbal abuse could be!

Kovary moved away from Cordero just long enough to raid the nightstand drawer and find the tube of lubricant and the box of condoms which he kept there.

"Safe sex only," Cordero gasped. He was so aroused, so short of breath, that he found it almost painful to speak. "I don't know you well enough to bareback. Okay?"

"Whatever you say," Kovary responded. "Your place, your rules. Just screw me. That's all I care about!"

His lust was contagious. A fever of eroticism, like an invisible flame, seemed to be passing back and forth between his naked body and Cordero's, raising their internal temperature, making them break out in a sweat. Cordero felt dizzy with desire as he twisted himself around toward the sexy cop on his bed so that he could look Kovary in the face.

"Please—let me suck you, sir," Cordero begged.

"Go ahead. You like being a prisoner, don't you? Like the way those cuffs feel? Makes you hot, doesn't it? Makes your dick drip and your ass hole twitch, huh?" Before Cordero could respond, verbally, to what was apparently a barrage of rhetorical questions, Kovary placed his hand on the back of his neck, and he none too gently pushed Cordero's down to his crotch. "Suck it all you want," the cop invited his captive.

Cordero went down on him, sucking his cock slowly and provocatively, exerting a maximum of pressure and friction, while Kovary reached for his chest and began working Cordero's nips again. Heat seemed to surge through Cordero's body. He was hot, and he desperately wanted to get the other guy hot, too—so hot that he'd follow through on his promise to open his ass hole and let Cordero fuck him like an animal!

"Now it's my ass hole that's twitching, stud," Kovary declared.

"Let me know when you're ready," Cordero panted, between licks on his cockhead.

"Oh, I'm ready—I'm ready right now! Don't tease me," he begged. "Just fuck me!"

Still licking his flesh, Cordero mumbled, "I need my hands free to do it."

"No, you don't."

Kovary tore open the condom's wrapper. Cordero's dick was so stiff that the cop seemed to have no trouble rolling the rubber down over it and securing it around the base of his shaft. Kovary smeared a generous quantity of the lube over the latex, and then he applied some more of the lubricant to his own erection—presumably that he could jerk it with a minimum of friction while he got fucked, if he so chose.

He took another glob of the gel and pressed it between his buttocks, working it onto and inside his puckered anal opening. During this operation, Cordero, observing intently, saw that the cop had a manly and very tempting ass hole, the sphincter surrounded by fine, fair hairs. The hole seemed to suck two of Kovary's fingers inside itself, and then it tightened against them and squirmed lewdly while he massaged the lube into his internal anal lining.

Kovary pulled his fingers out and helped Cordero to position himself on his knees on the mattress. He lay down on his back and spread his legs wide, placing them on either side of Cordero's hips.

"I guess we're ready," Kovary announced.

"I'm having trouble keeping my balance," Cordero complained when the mattress rocked slightly under the two men's combined weight.

"Oh, you look athletic enough to manage. Here, I'll help you. Stay put. Don't move yet. Yeah! Fuck me," the cop pleaded, bending his knees and lifting his legs high in the air, his face tense with erotic expectation. "In my hole," he invited Cordero. "Oh, get that big cock of yours in my hole!"

Kovary reached out, grasped Cordero's slippery, latex-sheathed dick, and jabbed it between his butt cheeks. Unable to use his hands, Cordero did his best to cooperate and help achieve the penetration. He pushed his sheathed dickhead between the man's parted ass cheeks, against the slicked-up sphincter. It entered easily, with some assistance from

Kovary's fingers, and another careful thrust inserted Cordero's erection all the way, so that his cock ring rubbed right up against the cop's manhole, which seemed to stick to the metal as though glued to it by the lube.

"There we go." As he spoke, the cop rolled his head to one side on the pillow and he groaned, his eyes closed.

"All right?" Cordero asked him, not moving his cock inside his body yet.

"Don't worry about me, I can take it. Just fuck! Use me. Fuck me as hard and as fast and as rough as you damn well want to, man, and go on fucking me until you come."

Cordero took him at his word. He didn't spare him! He fucked his hot cop ass with long, sharp jabs, pushing almost the entire length of his prick in and out of that butch butt, restraining himself only to the extent that he was careful not to let his cockhead slip out of his sex partner on the outward strokes.

It took a bit of trial and error on Cordero's part to keep himself poised on top of the other man without toppling over. But Kovary must have done this before. He encouraged Cordero to lean into it, hovering over the other man's torso, and Kovary pushed his knees back toward his shoulders, doubling himself up under Cordero's own body. At the same time, Kovary clasped Cordero's hips in his hands, steadying him.

The cop opened his eyes and stared up into his fucker's face. His mouth was open, his face flushed, his expression nothing short of ecstatic. The cop looked as though he was going to come right away!

"That's the way. Fuck me, fuck me," Officer Kovary repeated, over and over again. "Just stay there in the saddle and fuck! Come on, you goddamn Puerto Rican stud. Fuck me the same way you'd fuck a cunt. I've got my man pussy wide open for you, man. You know you like being in that hole! Oh,

God, keep your big, hard cock moving in and out of my ass, just like that!"

He was flexing his sphincter muscle, tilting his behind upward from the mattress and pressing it against Cordero's groin, wrapping his legs around his waist and using his hands to press down on Cordero's buttocks and drive his dick into him. He was doing everything in his power, in fact, which could possibly help Cordero to take him and to increase the intensity of the fuck. Cordero was astonished and pleased. This manly cop, this intrepid boy in blue, was behaving like the hottest gay whore in town!

It was a strange experience, to say the least. Cordero's wrists were secured behind his back. He couldn't touch himself, or the other man. He was the cop's prisoner. And yet the police officer was the one who was submitting to him, surrendering to him — giving up his hole to his captive.

"Fuck me!" Kovary yelled. "Copfuck me, dude! Copfuck me!"

None of Cordero's other sex partners had ever said *that*, in the heat of passion! He kind of liked the sound of it.

"I'll copfuck your stud ass, all right, goddamn you!" Cordero shouted back at him.

"Yeah!" Kovary roared.

He arched his back, pushing his pecs up, his tensed ab muscles quivering. His buttocks ground into Cordero's groin. Each time Cordero's prick drove deep into him, the glans seeking and nudging his prostate, Kovary groaned with delight.

Cordero's sweat fell from his face and dripped down onto the cop's face and chest. Cordero's hips pumped mechanically, in a slow but steady accelerando, speeding up his thrusts.

"Yeah — that's right," the cop whimpered. "Fuck me rough — hurt me — punish my ass!"

"You're a freaky fuck," Cordero taunted him.

"Just give me that dick," the other man begged, barely audible. "Big, hard dick in my ass!"

"Take it, you cop cunt!" Cordero raged.

The condom wasn't reducing his sensation or delaying his ejaculation in the slightest. If anything, it was making his prick feel more sensitive, more responsive to the friction which it was generating deep inside that ass.

Cordero tensed, leaned in more forcefully, breathed louder, humped harder, sweated more profusely—and he knew that he was about to come!

"Ah, Jesus, Mother of God," Cordero moaned. "Holy Christ! I'm going to blow," he warned his frantically aroused sex partner. "I'm going to come in your ass, cop!"

"Yeah!" the cop gasped. Cordero guessed the man felt Cordero's dick start to quiver inside him, filling the tip of the condom with his thick, hot sperm. "Oh—*yeah!*"

"Shit!" Cordero shouted.

"Shit!" the cop squealed, echoing him.

"Fucking hell!"

"God, oh, God, sweet Jesus!" Kovary blasphemed, writhing under Cordero's relentless anal onslaught.

Cordero finished coming. Then, at last, he stopped trying to keep his balance, allowing himself to topple clumsily over onto his side on his bed. The motion made him pull out of his bedmate, who seemed caught up in the grip of an overpowering lust, a raw sexual need which was almost frightening to watch.

Once again, Kovary's hand shot out and seized Cordero by the back of his neck. This time, roughly, he guided the boy's face to his chest.

"Bite my fucking nips. Bite them! Come on, sink your teeth in them. Do it hard—hurt me—make me come!" the cop begged, as he massaged his cock toward orgasm.

47

He gripped his shaft in his fist, which pumped up and down, and then with his other hand he reached down between his legs, where he found the ends of the insulated wire wrapped around his genitals, and he began to tug on them, like a puppeteer manipulating an obscene marionette—making his cock and balls bounce up and down, wildly, while he masturbated.

Meanwhile, Cordero obeyed, letting the guy push his head back and forth, urging him to sink his teeth into first one nipple, then the other, and then back again. It must've hurt like hell, but the cop seemed ecstatic. While he jerked himself with one hand, he caressed Cordero's head with the other, his fingers stroking through the strands of Cordero's disheveled, sweaty hair and massaging his scalp. There was an odd tenderness in the motions.

"Feels so good," Kovary reported, staring down at Cordero, wide-eyed, rapt with lust.

"You fucking freak," Cordero told him, between bites, although his tone of voice sounded more admiring than judgmental.

"No—no more!" Kovary screamed, shoving Cordero's head away from his chest and his tortured nipples.

The cop came quickly, his semen slashing across his hairy chest in thick, gleaming white streaks, like wet welts. Howling, he heaved and thrashed his way through his violent orgasm. Cordero was afraid the dude was going to hurt himself, he came so hard!

"Motherfucking hell," Kovary groaned, going limp.

"Are you all right?" Cordero inquired.

"I will be. Nothing like shooting out a big load of cum, is there?"

"Nothing, yeah," Cordero agreed.

"I knew you'd be like this, boy."

"Like what?"

"Kind of wild."

"And just how could you tell that, ahead of time."

Breathlessly, Kovary laughed. "Instinct, kid. Sheer instinct. I'm usually able to trust it."

"Ah, officer — please — my wrists?"

"Starting to hurt?"

"They're starting to go numb."

"Can't have that. Wait. Hold still."

After a moment, Kovary found his keys, and he used them to unlock the handcuffs. Cordero inspected the red indentations left on his wrists, rubbing them.

"Oh, God, I needed that," Kovary sighed, when he lay in Cordero's arms afterward, both of them recovering from their violent orgasms and enjoying the cuddling. "I needed that so bad! I thought I'd go crazy if I didn't come. Not by myself, though. It had to be another guy. A hot guy, like you!"

As though he was embarrassed, he fell silent, although he continued, mutely, to caress Cordero.

The police officer was a bundle of contradictions, no doubt, Cordero had begun to realize. On the job, Kovary probably played the part of the tough cop, stern, all business, although capable of lightening up and indulging in some humor, if the situation permitted that. When they were in Cordero's living room, drinking beer and talking, he was just one gay man interacting with another, without any pretense. In Cordero's bed, during the feverish frenzy of sex, he was a wild man, uninhibited — a dirty sex pig. And, as Cordero knew only too well, it took one to know one. As a shameless sex pig himself, he recognized a fellow porker when he wallowed in the mire with one! But now, in the aftermath of their lust, the cop was affectionate and sweet. And also kind of shy, which Cordero found endearing.

"Did you? Need that? Then I'm glad I was able to give it to you," Cordero told him.

"You like to fuck, obviously," he remarked.

"Who doesn't?"

"How'd you like plowing my ass?"

"The being handcuffed part was kind of strange. Other than that, it was fine," Cordero assured him, sincerely.

"Glad you liked it. Being cuffed didn't seem to cramp your style too much. I've been so tense lately, so goddamn uptight. I guess you've got the cure for that, though, buddy," Officer Kovary said. "A hot number like you — you must have a lot of fuck buddies," he suggested, looking and sounding slightly chagrined.

"Not *that* many," Cordero protested.

"Does that mean you can make room for me in your schedule?"

"I'm sure I'll be able to fit you in."

"Good. Listen — in all seriousness, no bullshit — can I come visit you again?"

"Sure," Cordero told him. "Any time you like. After all, we've got to keep each other out of trouble."

CHAPTER SIX: UNWINDING—AND RE-WOUND

Cordero realized that he still had the condom, its tip weighed down by his semen inside it, dangling from his deflated dick. No doubt he looked slightly ridiculous. Discreetly, he removed the used rubber and tied a knot in it, to keep its contents from leaking out, and then he deposited it on the nightstand.

His visitor didn't seem to notice the maneuver. Lost in thought, the cop also didn't appear to be in any hurry to depart.

"What we just did," Cordero inquired. "Would that be considered a bondage scene?"

The cop smiled. "A very light one. Nothing major." Suddenly, Kovary seemed to be in an expansive, even light-hearted, mood. "How'd you like being a sex slave?" he asked.

"Sex slave? *You* were the one who got fucked," Cordero reminded him.

"You were the one who was cuffed. I used your dick like a human dildo. Just a borrowed tool, to satisfy my ass."

That didn't strike Cordero as a flattering assessment, to say the least.

Kovary sat up on the bed, with his legs swung over its edge. Looking down, he inspected his groin.

"This is beginning to chafe." He began to untwist the wire from around his genitals. "Mind if I toss it?" he asked, indicating the wastebasket which Cordero kept in his bedroom.

"No, go right ahead." Cordero found the removal process quite intriguing to observe. Freed from Kovary's junk, the length of wire hit the inside of the wastebasket with a faint *thud.*

"Christ, I needed that fuck," Kovary confessed. "Bad."

"Did you?" Cordero asked.

"Yeah. Sex — good sex — that's what I needed, to unwind. Damn — after a day on the job, all I want to do is whip out my dick and blow my wad. Jerking off doesn't always do it for me. I'd much rather have some hot guy taking care of me. There's nothing like a real sex pig, when you need one."

Cordero was a bit annoyed. The cop kept saying how hard up *he'd* been, how tense and stressed — how badly *he'd* needed to unwind.

It's all about him. I suppose my feelings are unimportant. Good sex? Yeah — it was pretty good, I don't deny it. But convenience sex — that was probably more like it, judging by the way the dude keeps going on about how he needed relief.

"Glad I could oblige. I was better than a hand job, I suppose."

Kovary apparently detected the edge in Cordero's voice. "There's no need to be cynical."

"I'm not. Trying to be pleasant, sociable, that's all. Jesus, man, you're —"

"Unpleasant? Unsociable? I admit it," Kovary said. "I can be, at times."

"You needn't be so proud of it," Cordero suggested.

"I'm not. Occupational hazard, that's all. Well. I'd better get dressed, and go."

"Sure, if you're in a hurry to get away from me," Cordero said, tartly.

"I'm not in such a hurry," the cop said. "It's late, that's all. Give me your number."

Cordero gave Kovary his phone number. "Don't I get yours?"

"A top usually calls a bottom, not the other way around."

"Oh, I see. One of those *don't call me, I'll call you* situations, huh? The lord and master summons the serf, who's supposed to come running?"

Kovary smiled. "You're kind of mouthy, for a *serf*. But I like your balls. A guy who isn't afraid to stand up to me—yeah, that's a challenge. You don't like me very much, outside of the sack, do you?"

Taken aback by the cop's frankness, Cordero was at a loss for words. "Uh—"

"You hate my guts, I can tell. That's all right."

"I don't *know* you," Cordero said, by way of explanation.

"Maybe I'll grow on you, once you do." There was an almost flippant tone in Kovary's voice and an impish look on his face. He followed through by flashing Cordero an annoyingly seductive smile. "I'll call first, next time, instead of showing up uninvited," the police officer promised. "Okay?"

"Sure. That'll save you ringing the doorbell in vain, in case I'm not home."

The cop got dressed. Cordero put his boxers back on, in a gesture toward modesty. The policeman retrieved his handgun and slipped it back into its holster. He'd hidden the weapon on one of the living room windowsills, in between two of Cordero's potted houseplants, and behind the closed drapes—which was undeniably among the last places where Cordero would've looked.

Cordero escorted Kovary to the door, where, smiling somewhat enigmatically at him, the cop gave him a hug and kiss.

"I enjoyed tonight. Had a good time," the cop declared.

"Did you? So did I."

"I own you, now," Kovary boasted.

"Do you?" Cordero was dubious.

"Yeah. I own your ass, whether you're willing to admit it, or not."

"As you wish, officer."

"No, it's what *you* want, from now on, that's important."

"It's too late, and I'm too sleepy, for me to think clearly," Cordero pleaded. "I'm in no mood, no condition, to debate with you, man. Please."

"Yeah. Guess so. Take care," Kovary advised. "Try to stay out of trouble."

"You, too, officer," Cordero dared to retort.

The cop smiled. "I'm not the one we need to worry about." Then he was gone, stomping down the stairs.

After Kovary was gone, Cordero took another beer from his fridge, and he relaxed, drinking it. Realizing he really ought to get some sleep, he returned to his bedroom, where he shed his boxers.

He was about to get into bed when he remembered the wire in the wastebasket. Retrieving it, he did his best to reuse it to restraint his own genitals, trying to imitate the way it had looked — and no doubt felt — wound tightly around the cop's cock and balls.

Fucking hell! This feels hot — kind of weird, but hot. Really sexy! No wonder —

Suddenly, the realization hit Cordero. He didn't even know the police officer's first name! For that matter, he couldn't recall ever having told the cop his own name. They were such a pair of horn dogs that they'd gone at each other without bothering with the introductions.

No, wait. He took my ID the night we met. He looked at it. He saw my name and address. He must've memorized them. He knows damn well who I am. Which is kind of flattering, come to think of it. He must've already decided he wanted to see me again. He wanted me!

For sex — impersonal sex.

Just for that. Nothing else. He said so.

Sex, both of us scratching our itch, like animals!

Well, what the fuck? What else is there?

Nothing. Not much, anyway. Still — I can't help thinking — wishing —

He's such a hot fucking son of a bitch! Bastard. Sexy bastard. Full of himself, all right. Thinks he's too good for me. Stuck-up prick!

I hate his guts!

Well, as for discovering his elusive cop's first name, Cordero could rectify that omission, next time — assuming there'd be a next time. For all Cordero knew, despite Kovary having asked him whether he'd be interested in a rematch, this had been a one-shot deal.

Shit — just another one-night stand, to add to all the others. Whore! I'm nothing but a whore!

A dirty, lousy, cop-loving whore!

Closing his hand in a fist around his erection, Cordero began to masturbate, the wire biting into his swollen flesh.

Madness, sex madness. Irrational desire. There was no explanation for it, no logic to it.

CHAPTER SEVEN: GOOD WITH HIS TOOLS

Several days and nights passed. Cordero didn't hear from the elusive and provocative Officer Kovary, who had made such an ambiguous impression on him. Sullenly, Cordero assumed that the hot cop had just been toying with him.

Yeah, all that son of a bitch in uniform wanted from me was one night of sex.

I must've been crazy to get involved with him to begin with. So fuck him! Fuck all gay cops! To hell with them. Bastards — dirty, stinking bastards, I bet all of them are on the take!

Cordero enjoyed his wallow in resentful, erotic rage. It soothed him, somewhat.

One evening, after Cordero was done with his classes and work for the day, his buddy Riley called him and invited him to drop by his place.

Cordero, as Riley had no doubt anticipated, was quick to accept the invitation. The two guys hadn't gotten together for sex for a week or two. They were overdue. Cordero was eager for a rematch.

First, a man in blue. Now, a blue collar stud! It'll be interesting to compare them.

Cordero hoped that he wasn't a snob. Still, his friendship with Riley emphasized the importance of pursuing his education.

Riley was an excellent mechanic, which undeniably required some expertise. Otherwise, though, he perhaps wasn't the sharpest knife in the drawer, having by his own admission barely completed high school.

He lived in a frankly crummy, rundown, dirt-cheap studio apartment above a storefront. Cordero's own modest living quarters were palatial by comparison. Not that Riley was destitute. He owned both a pickup truck and a motorcycle, which were recent models and quite nice, although he probably saved some money by maintaining them himself. Still, insuring the vehicles must have taken a bite out of his income.

Riley was a fiery redhead, with pale, lightly freckled skin.

Obviously proud of his luxuriant head of flaming hair, he wore it long, tumbling down loosely below his shoulders. The long, thick, wavy locks were surely high-maintenance, and when he rode his bike, he had to restrain them under a bandana or a cap, to keep them from whipping about his head and getting in his face and his eyes. He restrained them similarly when he was on the job in the garage.

Cordero liked to see Riley when the dude had his hair down, both literally and figuratively. On such occasions, Riley resembled a Viking warrior stud, and he displayed an unabashed libido which went well with that savage image.

In addition to his flaming red mane, Riley also sported a mustache and a full beard, although he kept his facial hair neatly trimmed, shampooed, and combed.

The hot ginger stud, Cordero had soon learned, was a bit of a contradiction. Outwardly, Riley could look and act tough and hard, even rather mean. When he patronized a gay bar, or he cruised the streets of the city, this persona appealed to men who liked rough trade. Riley convincingly played the part of a brute, a hardcore fucker, a man born to satisfy the desires of submissive, masochistic gay men.

Like a good Irish-American Catholic boy, the mechanic wore a gold crucifix on a gold chain, slung around his sturdy, bull-like neck and his well-developed trapezius muscles, so that the crucifix nestled against his breastbone, in the deep groove between his hard, massive, hairy pecs. Riley rarely took off the necklace, wearing it in the gym, in the shower, and in bed—not just when he slept, otherwise naked, but also when he had sex. The small image of the Savior had witnessed some fairly shocking and lamentably sinful scenes.

In his free time, Riley's preferred mode of dress was biker style, heavy on black leather and blue denim. He wore comfortable old jeans, faded and softened by frequent washings, often with rips and tears in them. Sometimes when he went to a bar he wore black leather chaps, with the crotch and ass cut out to expose the denim underneath.

He favored tight-fitting T-shirts or tank tops as well, to show off his muscular torso. Motorcycle boots, of course, thick-soled, square-toed, with buckles. A denim jacket, or a black leather motorcycle jacket. A denim or black leather cap. Outdoors, during the daytime, while driving his pickup or riding his bike, dark glasses, hiding his eyes and giving him a vaguely sinister look. His accessories tended to be bandanas, and a black leather belt, wristbands, and armbands, studded or spiked, and chrome chains, with rings, neck pendants, and bracelets featuring crosses or skulls.

Riley liked to taunt Cordero by calling him, variously, *college boy*, *jock*, or *white bread*. Wincing in response to these dismissive descriptions, Cordero strove to prove to Riley that he was more than any of those things, and that he could meet the man on his own crude terms. Riley liked his sex partners to be masculine, and while Cordero was hardly fem, he did consciously do everything in his power to butch himself up whenever he and Riley got together for sex.

Cordero had received quite a surprise the first time he saw Riley naked.

The long-haired, bearded ginger's earlobes, nipples, and navel were pierced, with heavy-gauge surgical steel rings inserted in them. Riley had a guiche in his perineum muscle, between his balls and his ass hole. He had an eyebrow piercing, and — what the somewhat naïve Cordero found most startling of all — a Prince Albert piercing in his cockhead. The thought of having that pierced and ringed dick shoved in his mouth, down his throat, and up his ass had at first intimidated Cordero. But he'd quickly gotten used to feeling the heavy-gauge metal ring in his various orifices.

Furthermore, the guy was heavily tattooed, with Celtic tribal designs on his torso, the ink adorning large areas of his shoulders, back, chest, and arms. Whether he was attired in his biker gear, or he was naked, Riley was a formidable-looking sight.

Underneath this exaggeratedly butch veneer, however, he could be a perfectly amiable, easygoing guy.

Riley had a healthy sex appetite which matched Cordero's own, and a total lack of inhibition. Being in bed with him tended to turn into a nude wrestling match, culminating after a great deal of grappling in the mutual goal of orgasm.

In the single long, rectangular main room of Riley's studio apartment, Cordero sat down next to his friend on his broken-down old couch, near the unmade bed. The two men drank beer, with which Riley was always well-supplied.

"What's new on campus, college boy?" Riley teased Cordero. "You been fucking a lot of those other jocks?"

"Not as many as I'd like," Cordero retorted.

"Frustrated, huh? Hard up?"

"A little."

"Well, you've come to the right place. I've been just about busting to drop a load, too." With a beer can in one hand, Riley used the other nonchalantly to rub his crotch through his well-worn, stained jeans. "Yeah, my balls are in an uproar. Come on, let's fuck."

"Before we do that, let me ask you something. Remember how you're always trying to talk me into trying some of that

BDSM stuff?" Cordero inquired.

"Sure. But it was just talk. You know, a suggestion. I wouldn't want you to do anything you couldn't get into."

"Guys like it when you top them?"

Riley smirked. "Never heard any complaints. Of course, sometimes the dude has a gag in his mouth, so he's not exactly in a position to do any goddamn whining."

"Well, maybe I've changed my mind. I wouldn't mind giving it a try—in moderation. You know, just enough to get an idea of what it's like."

"Oh, really? What brought this on?"

"I met this guy, who got a little rough with me."

"Oh? Anybody I know?"

"I doubt it." Evasively, Cordero didn't volunteer any information about the *guy's* identity, and Riley didn't press the issue.

Riley seemed more interest in hearing about the sex. "Rough as in you liked it, or rough as in you didn't like it?"

"I liked it a lot. He handcuffed me. He got kind of verbal with me. Told me what to do."

"Sounds hot."

"It was."

Riley grinned. "Put ideas into your head, huh? Opened your eyes to the possibilities? Want to give it a try here tonight, with me?"

"Yeah."

The truth was, Cordero had been contemplating this possibility ever since he'd received his friend's phone call, inviting him to come to his place.

Cordero had promptly begun fantasizing, working himself up into a state of feverish arousal and erotic anticipation. He saw himself as anxious to report for duty at Riley's apartment, eager to submit to his demands and do anything which Riley wanted from him, no matter how perverse. Cordero would be a bottom, a submissive, a cock whore. Once again, he would experience the strange thrills which Officer Kovary had given him. Cordero suspected that Riley might be a more than adequate substitute, as a top. Cordero would obey him, and service him without question or hesitation, no matter how disgusting and humiliating the demands Riley might make on him. Cordero would be his obedient, submissive little bitch!

"So—how do we get started?" Cordero asked.

"Well, first we need to give you a safe word." Riley spoke in a businesslike manner, as though they were discussing which part was need for an automobile repair. "A code word. What you say when you want me to stop. I know. *Socket wrench*. You just say *socket wrench* if things start to get too much for you. Then, you see, the top has an absolute obligation to stop. No delay, no two questions about it, no bullshit."

"I see." Cordero was rather impressed. Kovary hadn't mentioned anything about a safe word or phrase. Maybe Riley was more sophisticated than Cordero had given him credit for.

Setting his beer can down, Riley rose from the couch and moved toward the bed. Cordero followed him.

"When I let a bottom take care of me, I don't put up with any attitude or bullshit from him," Riley warned.

"Yes, sir," Cordero whimpered.

"That means I expect nothing less than total, unquestioning obedience."

"Of course, sir."

Riley grunted. "So far, so good. Maybe you've got the makings of a first-rate slave boy, after all. We'll soon see. *Cunt*," he added insultingly. "You're here for one thing, and one thing only. I've got a big old hard-on, right here in my pants. Which means I can probably shoot more than once tonight, but first, I'm in the mood for a quickie. I feel like dropping a load right off the bat. Come on. Take care of that for me, college boy," Riley said. "Right now!"

Naturally, it didn't occur to him to ask what Cordero might be in the mood for or feel like doing. Cordero was the bottom. He was there to satisfy Riley, without hesitation or question, like a sex appliance which could be switched on and off at will.

Sure of his sex partner's compliance, Riley stripped out of his clothes, and he lay down on the bed. Staring at his pierced and tattooed body, admiring it, desiring it, Cordero also undressed, and joined him on the bed.

"Start off by licking me a little," Riley requested, in a stern tone of voice which allowed no room for refusal.

Cordero began licking the redhaired man all over his body—his neck, his shoulders, his well-developed, pumped-up pectoral muscles, his nipples, his armpits, his stomach, all the way down past his navel and his thick red pubic bush, to his groin, which smelled of sweat and leather. Running his tongue through the hair, he next rubbed his tongue down over the fat uncircumcised cock and the balls, before lapping hungrily at Riley's thighs.

He made his way to Riley's feet, which also smelled of leather. Passionately, Cordero sucked on the mechanic's toes and licked the soles of his feet. Then he ran his tongue back up the man's legs, and he pushed them into the air so that he could begin sucking his ass. He pressed his lips to the puckered anal opening in a wet kiss, worked his tongue in circular motions over the pliable, flexing pink flesh of the sphincter, and then he flexed his tongue in and out, fucking Riley's ass hole with it. Riley was masturbating himself while Cordero rimmed him.

"Get down on my cock," Riley said, hoarsely. "I want to shoot my load. In your mouth."

Easing Riley's legs back down onto the bed, Cordero

jammed his head down into his groin and his lips seized the guy's swollen, pierced prick. The Prince Albert scraped over his lips and tongue.

"Yeah, that's the way, kid," Riley gasped, as Cordero fed the whole length of the hotly pulsing dick into his mouth. "Give it a good suck. You suck that thing good and hard, like the dirty little cocksucker you are, and I'll let you have a nice big load."

Cordero bobbed his head up and down as he mouthed the throbbing prick. By now, he was accustomed to coping with the additional challenge which Riley's Prince Albert presented to a cocksucker. Cordero tickled and massaged and tugged on Riley's balls with one hand while he worked a finger of his other hand into the cleft between Riley's buttocks and inside his ass. Sucking and finger-fucking, he breathed through his nose, and he managed to suppress his gag reflex and slide his lips all the way down on the shaft of the thick cock, taking the pierced and ringed glans into his throat.

"Yeah, keep it up just like that," Riley moaned. "Keep going. Suck that dick and finger that hole."

Cordero could feel Riley's cock swelling larger inside his mouth, the tide of his sperm rising to a flood. Suddenly, Riley let out a groan, and his cock erupted, spewing hot jets of creamy semen down his cocksucker's throat. Cordero swallowed the torrent, smacking his lips and grunting to express his delight at being so well-fed, as he drank up every drop of Riley's potent fluid.

"Shit," Riley declared, happily. "You're getting better at that, all the time. I just might have to keep you around. A good cum dump is hard to find, and it always comes in handy. Now," he said, in a stern, authoritative tone of voice. "Give me a tongue bath. All over my naked body. Lick the sweat off me. Get your mouth going on my ink, I want to feel your fucking tongue scrubbing my tattoos. Get my dick good and hard again, and then I'll shove it up your ass. I can come again, for sure. Yeah, boy, I'm going to fuck you raw, and breed and seed your hole. And you're going to love it. You'll be begging me for more."

Cordero didn't doubt it!

"But wait," Riley gasped. In his lingering post-ejaculatory excitement, he was short of breath. "You liked being hand-cuffed, huh?"

"Yeah. I mean, yes, sir," Cordero admitted, humbly. "I liked it a lot!"

Riley slid open the drawer of the small nightstand beside his bed. "Got something just as good here." He rummaged among the items in the drawer, and he pulled out the sort of disposable plastic tie which had a tab which could be threaded through an opening so that the tie could be drawn tight and locked.

Such an object had all sorts of utilitarian uses, but Cordero knew that cops often carried them, so they could restrain mul-tiple detainees if they ran out of metal handcuffs. He felt a hot surge of lust ripple through him as Riley bound his wrists be-hind his back with the tie, securing it very tightly, the plastic band digging into his flesh.

"Nice and tight," Riley declared, with satisfaction. "Now you're my property. Not going anywhere."

"Yes, sir," Cordero whimpered. Riley's property, just as he'd been Kovary's!

Naked – a prisoner – can't use my hands, can't fight back, can't resist!

Next, Riley took a pocket knife from the drawer and opened its blade. "We'll need this to cut you loose, when I'm done with you." He leered. "Which won't be for a while. I'm going to edge you, boy, and I'm going to take things good and slow, work up to it gradually until I'm ready to come again. Then I'll blow off another big wad."

Finally, Riley removed a fresh bottle of liquid poppers

from the drawer. He peeled off the cellophane wrapper around its top and unscrewed the cap. He held the small brown bottle up to his nose, pinching one nostril shut while he inhaled through the other. After taking several hits on each side of his nose, he made Cordero sniff the amyl fumes, which quickly went to Cordero's head, giving him a strong rush. Lightheaded, Cordero seemed to feel the tawdry room spinning around him, and an intense sexual heat spread through his bound body.

"Yeah," Riley grunted. "Get you good and high, slave, so you'll do anything I tell you to do. No matter how dirty! This is going to be fun. Shit—shouldn't have waited so long to do it! Going to make up for all that lost time now."

Chapter Eight: Reporting a Crime

Cordero had kept the length of electrical wire, as a souvenir, coiling it and placing it in his bureau drawer.

Desperately, Cordero longed to give himself to Kovary again. Submitting to his crude fuck buddy Riley had only whetted Cordero's appetite, and made him eager to make further explorations in the frightening yet thrilling world of BDSM.

In his more sane moments, Cordero had questioned his obsession.

Cordero had suspected, cynically, with resignation, that all Officer Kovary wanted from him was a one-night stand. But he was wrong about that. One Monday evening, about a week after his memorable hookup with Riley, Cordero received a phone call.

"Yeah?" he asked.

"It's me—your friendly neighborhood law enforcement."

Cordero recognized the voice. It had that silken insinuation in its timbre, which was instantly dick-hardening to hear. A hot rush of sexual anticipation swept through him.

"Oh, it's you, Officer Kovary," Cordero replied, trying to sound as casual as possible, but, he feared, no doubt failing miserably in the attempt. "Nice to hear from you again."

"Is it? Does that mean you're no longer pissed off at me?"

"Ah—who said I was ever—"

"I got the impression our hookup the other night was kind of lacking in romance, for you."

"I didn't think *romance* entered into it at all. Which was

fine. If you ask me, officer, romance is overrated."

Kovary chuckled. "I have to agree. It usually is. How was your weekend?"

"Okay. Routine."

"Did you get laid?" the police officer asked, bluntly.

"Ah, no, I didn't, as a matter of fact." *Unless you count jacking off a couple of times, while I was thinking about you.* That was what Cordero was tempted to say. *Thinking about how fucking hot you looked in your uniform — and out of it! Wishing I had your cuffs on my wrists. And your cop dick in my mouth and up my ass!* But he restrained himself. He didn't want to scare off this enigmatic stud by behaving like too much of a whore.

"My weekend was pretty dull," Kovary said. "And short. I had to pull a shift yesterday. Not my favorite way to spend a Sunday. Want some company?"

"Sure."

"I'll be right over."

"Wait. Before we get intimate again—"

"Yeah?"

"I think we should be properly introduced. What's your first name, Officer Kovary?"

"Oh, that's right. We never got around to that, did we?"

"No, we didn't. While we're on the subject—Kovary, is that a Polish name? Or Czech?"

Kovary scoffed, "Don't they teach you, college boys, anything nowadays? About geography? About history? About different nationalities? For your information, it's Hungarian."

"Oh. Sorry. Hey, how'd you know I go to college?"

"Just a wild guess. It was written all over you. Typical college guy—"

Cordero caught the faint hint of contempt in Kovary's voice, but he chose to ignore it.

"I see. And your first name, Officer Kovary? Can't I know it?" *Or is that somehow against the BDSM rules, too?*

"It's Emeric."

"Unusual."

"Not so much so, at least not in Hungary. It's an old Germanized form of Imre, which is one of the most common Hungarian men's names. My parents were traditionalists. Nostalgic for the old country."

"It suits you. But what do your friends call you? Ric?"

"They call me Emeric. And you can address me as *sir*, or *officer*. For the time being. When I want to get more intimate with you—verbally, that is—I'll let you know."

"Oh. All right, sir."

"I didn't call you to discuss the fine points of nomenclature, if that's the right word for it."

"I believe it is."

Officer Emeric Kovary. So that was his name. It had a certain ring to it. But no doubt he was a mere mortal, not a sex god. He surely had feet of clay.

He's nothing but a man, like other men. Nothing extraordinary about him. That was what Cordero stubbornly told himself. *So what if he's hot? If he's good-looking? If he's built? If he's hung? So what? Lots of guys are hot, good-looking, built, and hung. Uh, big-dicked cop bastard! Like a goddamn porn star! Huh, Emeric Kovary—sounds like one of those Hungarian porn actors!*

If only I could forget all about him. If only I could tell him to fuck off, right now, over the phone! Yeah, that might take him down a peg or two. But, no. No such luck.

Aw, fuck, I can't help it, can't help myself! I want that cop's cock in me, in my mouth, in my ass! Using me. Fucking me. Cop dick, dominating me, making me his bitch! Damn, oh, damn!

"Still there?" Kovary asked.

"Uh, yeah. My thoughts kind of wandered, for a moment. Sorry."

"Guess I'm not much of a conversationalist. I don't mean to bore you."

"You're not. In fact—"

"Yes?"

"Well, Officer Emeric Kovary, sir, I'd like to report a crime which is about to take place here in my neighborhood."

"What sort of a crime?"

"A sex crime. I'm about to start jerking off," Cordero confessed. "And blow my wad all over the place. Which *would* be a crime — a waste. Maybe you could come over here and catch the perpetrator in the act and stop him. You can take charge of the situation and show him that there are — certain alternatives."

"Sounds like an emergency. I'll be right there."

"Hurry," Cordero urged him. "Sir," he remembered to add.

"I'll turn on the lights and the siren," Emeric promised. Cordero assumed he was joking. The fantasy of having a horny cop tear through traffic in a patrol car in his impatience to hook up with him was definitely arousing, though. "See you soon."

His cop acquaintance had hung up. *Acquaintance* — was that the right word to describe him? Cordero wasn't sure. *Boyfriend, lover* — those terms were definitely premature. *Sex partner, fuck buddy* — blunt-sounding, maybe, but accurate enough. *Fucker!* That was even cruder, but it also seemed to fit. *That's right. Officer Emeric Kovary is my fucker!* There was a flash of defiance in Cordero, as he acknowledged that fact. *Fucker, my fucker. Yeah, I let him fuck my ass!*

Emeric Kovary — now I know what to call him. The name really does have a kind of porn actor ring to it. Sounds like one of those Eastern European guys who does gay porn! Some of them are really straight, and just gay for pay, supposedly. But not my cop fucker. Nothing straight about him!

Cordero prepared to receive his visitor by unzipping his jeans and pushing them down, along with his boxers so that he could put on his cock ring. Then he zipped himself up again. Cordero had long ago discovered that there was a certain unique mental state a guy entered into when he was looking forward to a sexual sure thing. His mental reservations were on *hold*, while his physical responses took over, dominating him. Cordero's pulse accelerated. He was already breathing harder and perspiring. His whole being was preparing itself for sex. As the saying went, he was truly doing all of his thinking not with his brain, but with his stiff dick!

Twenty minutes later, Emeric Kovary was in Cordero's apartment, and they were embracing and kissing. Once again, the cop was in uniform, obviously having come to Cordero's place directly from work.

"I'll go into the kitchen and get us something to drink," Cordero said, "while you find a new hiding place for your gun."

Emeric grinned. "You remembered that, huh?"

"I've remembered everything about our previous get-together. It's not as though — "

"What?"

"It's not as though something like that happens to me every day."

"I made an impression on you, did I? I hope it was a good one."

"Let's just say you're a credit to the department. Serve and protect, as they say. You were especially good at the servicing part of it. Now, what'll you have? I was about to relax over a glass of cheap red wine when you called, but I'm well-stocked with other hooch. Including beer, of course."

"I'll join you in the wine, if I may. Cheap can have its charms."

"Is that a dig?"

Emeric grinned. "Consider it a compliment."

"Okay. Wine, coming right up."

When Cordero returned to the living room with the opened bottle of Montepulciano d'Abruzzo and two glasses, his guest was sitting on the couch, minus his pistol. Cordero sat beside him, poured the wine, and they drank.

"It was kind of funny, on the phone before," Emeric remarked. "You know, our discussion of ethnic origins. I don't know how we got sidetracked into that. You're Puerto Rican, aren't you?"

Like a lot of non-Spanish speakers, he mispronounced *Puerto* as *Porto*, which Cordero always found irritating. However, Cordero wisely didn't say so.

"That's right," he told his visitor. "It's obvious, I suppose."

"Um, not necessarily. You're not as dark as some."

"Is that good or bad?"

"Just making a remark. An observation. Don't be offended."

"I'm not. I've been told that, as we *PRs* go, I'm not bad-looking." Cordero spoke with a hint of bitterness. It was time to change the subject. "Arrest anybody today?" Cordero asked the policeman, in a tone of voice which was perhaps a bit flippant.

"Yeah, I did, actually. It wasn't all that dramatic. Shoplifter. Stealing items to sell to support his drug habit, no doubt. The damn fool was caught on tape on the store's video cameras. I'll have to show up in court in due course to testify. Business as usual. Tedious."

"Was he hot?" Cordero inquired.

Emeric laughed. "Now, *there's* a question that only a gay man would ask! Hot? Sort of. Depends on your taste, or your lack of it. He was a pumped-up, hopped-up, prison tattooed young scumbag. I suppose a guy who was desperate might get off on throwing a fuck into him."

"There's a hot fantasy," Cordero suggested. "Busting a guy—putting him in cuffs. Tossing his ass into a jail cell. And then going into the cell yourself and screwing him."

"Some imagination you've got there."

"But you must occasionally arrest guys whom you find attractive," Cordero said.

"Yeah, that happens. Occasionally, as you just said."

"When you cuff a hot guy and haul his ass downtown and book him—does that ever turn you on? Do you want to rape his ass and make him submit to you?"

"Sometimes," Emeric admitted. "I've been known to spring a boner. Which professionalism forces me to ignore. What about you? Ever fantasized about being cuffed and worked over by a cop?"

"I don't have to fantasize about it. I experienced it, the last time you were here, remember?"

"Oh, that was just a taste," Emeric said, dismissively. "Vanilla sex, really. On a scale of one to ten, maybe a three! But you liked it, did you?"

"I didn't dislike it," Cordero responded warily. "I'm starting to think about it right now, remembering what we did. The *being worked over* part doesn't appeal that much to me. I can get into a little rough sex, now and then, but not *too* rough. The cuffed part—that's different. Just the thought of it is kind of hot."

"Want to give it another try?"

"Yeah. Ever since I met you—I've been sort of thinking about that. What it might be like, if we did it again—and maybe went a little farther," Cordero blurted out, lustfully. "Shit! I guess I'm kind of a pervert."

"No, just adventurous. Open-minded. Finish your wine," Emeric urged him.

Cordero lost no time in draining his glass.

"Stand up," the cop instructed him. "And strip! And that's an order, perp!"

"Yes, sir. I'm prepared to be cooperative."

"Whether you cooperate or not, you're going to be in my custody," Emeric blustered.

Cordero got naked, fast.

"Sir," he murmured, doing his best to look and act humble. "Shouldn't we—"

"Quiet. Technically, you should speak to a dom, a top, only when spoken to. I'm prepared to make certain allowances, though, because you're a beginner. Did you want to ask me something? If so, you have my permission to speak," the cop deigned to say.

"Thank you, sir. What I wanted to say, was, shouldn't we have a safe word?"

"You're right. We were careless about that, last time. It's important that you know you can trust me. What'd you say before? *Protect and serve*? We'll use that. Easy for you to remember. *Protect and serve*. Now, turn around," Emeric commanded, taking his handcuffs from his belt. "Hands on top of your head—" Deftly, standing behind Cordero, he fastened his wrists behind his back. The steel hoops of the handcuffs felt cold against Cordero's skin. Stepping up even closer behind him, so that the front of his uniform shirt made contact with Cordero's bare back, Emeric reached around him with both arms.

With his left hand, he fondled Cordero's pecs and nipples, stroking them with his thumbs. "Yeah," he grunted when he felt Cordero's nips stiffen in response to his touch. "Nice chest, nice nips. Responsive. The kind I like." Still toying with them, he dropped his right hand to his prisoner's groin, grasping his cock and balls, hefting them, squeezing them. Cordero's dick was extremely rigid. The cop's fingers touched Cordero's cock ring and rotated it. "Hot," Emeric breathed into his ear. "I can tell you're the incorrigible type, though. A lost cause, a real career criminal! I think I'm going to enjoy fucking your punk ass. But first—I've got something I want to do with this big Puerto Rican dick of yours."

"Whatever you say, officer."

"You're damn right. Whatever I say, goes. You resist me, and you'll regret it. Now, march!"

Prodding Cordero from behind, Emeric had him precede him into his bedroom.

"Get your butt on the bed," Emeric barked, unceremoniously giving Cordero a push in that direction. With his hands fastened behind him, Cordero had a little trouble clambering onto the mattress. Finally, he more-or-less tumbled down on it, and he rolled over, onto his side, so that he could face the cop as he stood beside the bed.

"Come on," Cordero pleaded. "Don't be so rough."

"Shut the fuck up. I'll get as rough with you as I damn well please."

"Don't hurt me."

"I won't hurt you, unless you say or do something to piss me off. Then, I'll have to punish you. I may have to hurt you, real bad."

"Jesus," Cordero moaned.

"Jesus isn't here to save your ass, boy," Emeric taunted Cordero. "No, your butt belongs to me!"

"You're a—"

"What? What am I?"

"Nothing."

"Thought better of mouthing off to me, huh? Now you're acting smart. Don't make me have to hurt you. Be smarter than that. I'm so evil when I get angry," Emeric warned. "I can be—so cruel."

Cordero didn't doubt it!

Excitedly, Cordero watched the cop while he stripped. Emeric took his time about it, teasing him. When he was naked, Cordero saw that he wasn't wearing the kind of improvised electrical-wire genital restraint he'd sported during their previous encounter. Instead, he had on a metal cock ring quite similar to Cordero's own. It looked good on him. His erect prick, jutting out above his swollen balls, looked enormous!

"Lie down, on your back," Emeric instructed Cordero. "I'm going to edge you. Don't even think about resisting!"

"I wouldn't dream of it, sir," Cordero replied obediently.

He lay on his back with his cuffed hands resting rather uncomfortably between the mattress and the small of his back. Emeric straddled his thighs, leaning forward so that their cocks came into exciting contact.

Emeric licked his chin, his throat, his pecs. His tongue swabbed Cordero's armpits, tickling him. Cordero groaned with delight when the cop started to work on his nipples, using his mouth to suck on one hard tit, rubbing his saliva over the stiff brown cone, while his fingers teased its twin.

After he had serviced each of Cordero's nipples in that way, Emeric attacked his armpits again, more aggressively this time, licking them, breathing hard and moaning as though the taste of Cordero's sweat on his tongue and the smell of his overheated flesh in his nostrils had intoxicated him. He even caught Cordero's tufts of armpit hair in his teeth and pulled on them, while his hands pressed against Cordero's chest muscles and massaged his pecs again.

Cordero was desperate with lust by the time Emeric slid down his torso. After dipping his tongue-tip into Cordero's navel, the cop shoved his head between his thighs, and he began to lick and suck on Cordero's balls, coaxing both fat orbs inside his wet lips at once and slurping on them with loud, obscene greed.

Cordero's prick was so stiff by then that it was absolutely inflexible. When Emeric, still mouthing his testicles, grabbed the shaft, he could bend it only slightly. Letting Cordero's nuts slip wetly out of his mouth, he had to raise his head to get his tongue on the bloated dickshaft.

He wet it thoroughly with his saliva, and then he laid his

flushed cheek on Cordero's thigh and, with his head in that position, he simply opened his mouth and pushed the middle section of the cockshaft between his lips, as though he was eating an ear of steamed corn on the cob.

He moved his mouth back and forth to caress Cordero's cock from its base to its tip in this novel fashion, his lips and tongue curling around the meaty shaft, never actually taking the head of the penis inside his mouth. Simultaneously, he used one hand to tickle Cordero's balls, and his other hand to part his ass cheeks and penetrate his sphincter rim with a fingertip.

Cordero's thoughts raced. *Shit! If this is being dominated, being worked over by a top, then I'm all for it! The bastard's servicing me, not the other way around. But it's almost too goddamn intense. I'm getting too fucking hot, too turned on. This is like torture, sex torture!*

"I can't stand this," Cordero confessed, breathlessly, after several minutes of the delightful torture. "I'm going to have to come!"

"That's too damn bad," Emeric mumbled, with his lips still pressed against Cordero's steely phallic column. "Because I'm not going to let you come yet. You'll shoot when I damn well decide you're going to!"

"Now, listen here, cop!" Cordero blustered.

"Shut the fuck up." Emeric punctuated the command by delivering a sharp, stinging slap to Cordero's bare butt.

He resumed edging Cordero. He'd coax and goad him close to ejaculation, only to back off every time he sensed that Cordero was about to explode. After a few more minutes of this treatment, Cordero was in erotic agony. He writhed about on the bed, trying to escape from the man's tormenting mouth and hands. He tugged at the handcuffs, trying to free his wrists. All this was in vain, of course.

"Shit, officer, I'm so hard up, I ache so bad, it hurts!" he lamented. "Have some mercy, dude!"

Not deigning to reply, the sadistic cop went right on mouthing his prickshaft, still refusing actually to take it inside his mouth and suck on it. He tickled Cordero's balls relentlessly, and with his other hand he continued to probe between his prisoner's clenched buttocks, penetrating his ass hole now with three fingers, which he inserted inside Cordero as deeply as possible. Working them rapidly back and forth within the tight clasp of the spasming anus, he finger-fucked Cordero without letup.

Gritting his teeth, Cordero prayed for the relief which only orgasm could bring him.

At last, Emeric's teasing became too much for his overexcited body to endure. Cordero felt his piss slit gape wide open, burning, as though he needed to piss but he couldn't. A drop of pre-cum dripped from the opening. Noticing it, Emeric swiped it away with his tongue, and even that light, fleeting pressure on his cockhead made Cordero shiver from head to foot with lustful frustration. Next, he actually emitted a tiny squirt of semen. Emeric lapped up that, as well.

"Oh, God!" Cordero whimpered. "I'm going to come, you son of a bitch! And this time, there's nothing you can do to stop me!"

He wasn't exaggerating. It was no idle boast. He could already feel the sperm pressure peaking within him. As though a safety valve had suddenly opened, he felt a tingling sensation rushing through the core of his cock. His sperm was headed toward the exit!

Quick as a flash, Emeric abandoned his lip lock on Cordero's dick and his fingering of his ass. He repositioned himself, once again straddling Cordero's thighs so that he could grasp his cock in his right hand, his own cock in his left hand, and — holding both tools close together — he began to beat them both off.

"Come," he gasped, looking down at Cordero, wild with

excitement. "Go ahead and come! Shoot, goddamn you! Shoot! Give me that cum!"

He was masturbating Cordero with just the right amount of pressure, and at just the right pace, to encourage his ejaculation, instead of impeding it, as he'd done up until now. Cordero knew that he wasn't going to have any trouble blowing his wad, and so he sat up slightly and stared at his sex partner. Their eyes darted about restlessly. Neither of the two men seemed able to decide which was the more exciting thing to watch—the other guy's face, taut with pleasure and fast-approaching ecstasy, or their two dicks, being stroked so energetically in such close proximity between their bodies.

Their metal cock rings banged together, producing a clicking sound each time they met.

Cordero could see the tip of his dick getting wet again. Emeric rubbed the ball of his thumb over Cordero's gaping piss slit to capture the oozing semen and utilize it as a lubricant for his steadily pumping hand.

"Oh, I'm close," Cordero warned him. "I'm there—"

"All over me, man," Emeric insisted. "Blast your fucking jizz all over me!"

"Yours, too—I want yours on me, too!"

"Don't worry, you're going to get it! Fuck—aw, fuck!" the cop shouted.

He came first, to Cordero's surprise, throwing his head back and rearing up on his knees, his buttocks tightening to provide the impetus behind his spurts of hot wet sperm. He drenched Cordero's sweaty torso with his first few wads. But he'd beaten Cordero to the finish line by no more than a few seconds. Helplessly, Cordero lost his own load, his semen escaping from his hard-fisted prick in such quantities that the discharge resembled a single, sustained seminal hemorrhage rather than a series of individual bursts.

"Oh, Jesus!" Emeric cried out as they finished coming together. He let go of their wet, slippery pricks and grabbed his captive by his shoulders, his soiled fingers leaving slimy streaks on Cordero's flesh.

He kissed Cordero, passionately, as though he'd been starved for physical contact with another man, and he was now determined to make up for lost time.

"I really needed that," he said, by way of explanation, when they lay together afterward, with Emeric holding Cordero in a loose, sweaty embrace. "How do your wrists feel?"

"They're all right."

"Good." He grinned. "Maybe I won't uncuff you, then. Not just yet. I'm not done with you. Where do you keep the rubbers and the lube?"

"Right there, in the top drawer of the nightstand."

"I believe you forgot to say *sir*," Emeric coached Cordero.

"Yes, sir. I'm sorry, sir."

"I've been lax, letting you get away with mouthing off to me, disrespecting me. We'll have to be a little more rigorous about such things from now on." Emeric slid open the drawer. "I'm going to fuck the hell out of you, while you still have those cuffs on, and you aren't going to be able to resist," he vowed, in his toughest, most authoritative cop tone of voice. "You'd better be ready to give me that hole of yours."

"Yes, sir!"

"And don't even *think* of trying to resist."

"No, sir."

"I expect nothing less than complete submission."

"Complete submission, yes, sir. Nothing less."

CHAPTER NINE: TWO COPS FOR THE PRICE OF ONE

Cordero had difficulty concentrating on his school work. He was easily distracted by erotic speculations. A favorite pastime of his was trying to decide which of his classmates and fellow athletes he'd like to recruit for BDSM experiments, if he could have his pick of them. Even some of his professors played starring roles in his porn-like fantasies!

He decided he especially liked Joel, the captain of the college's soccer team, to which Cordero belonged. Joel was presumably unattainable because he had a reputation on campus as a ladies' man. In the yearbook, he ought to be labeled as *Most likely to get a girl knocked up*. Furthermore, he was a yuppie-ish type who came from a prominent, wealthy family. He was always perfectly polite to Cordero, but the two young men moved in different social circles, and they could hardly be called friends.

Joel's main qualification as fantasy fodder was the fact that he was a handsome, muscular blond guy, who, to Cordero's way of thinking, resembled a younger version of Emeric Kovary.

Fantasy was one thing. Reality was another, and ultimately much more satisfying. Cordero really didn't need to settle for a facsimile of Emeric. Not when he could have the real thing!

Cordero was always happy to get a phone call from Emeric because he knew it was the prelude to another hot, thoroughly enjoyable hookup. The cop was predictable, in the best sense of the word!

Subtly, though, their relationship had changed. Emeric seemed more comfortable in Cordero's company. He allowed himself to relax, saving his stern demeanor for when the two of them were involved in an actual BDSM scene. Otherwise, he could be quite amiable. He even let Cordero get away with mouthing off to him, teasing him — within reason.

"Still got those marks on your butt where I beat your ass with my belt?" Emeric inquired.

"They've faded," Cordero told him. "And I can actually sit down again, without wincing."

"Good. Want to get together on Friday night?" Emeric asked him.

"Sure. My place, as usual?"

"That'll work. Tell me something, though — do you like threesomes?"

"Love them," Cordero admitted.

"Something told me you might," the police officer said, rather cynically. "How'd you like to fuck around with me — *and* another cop? Another top, like me?"

Cordero had to laugh. "What I like about you, Officer Kovary, is that you're so direct. No beating around the bush for you! Two cops at once? Wow! That sounds like it could really be something." But then a thought occurred to him. "Wait. You're not talking about your partner, are you? Donut Boy? The guy you were cruising around with in the patrol car, the night we met?"

"How dare you refer to a police officer as *Donut Boy*. What we have here is a lamentable lack of respect for the law." But then Emeric laughed. "No, not him, although guys who are carrying around a few extra pounds need love, too. But he's straight. I'm thinking about another cop I know, a good buddy of mine. Trust me, he's hot. Although, speaking of prejudices — if you don't like chubbies, then how do you feel about fit-bodied, well-hung men who just happen to be black?"

"Do I look like the kind of guy who'd be prejudiced about skin color? You've seen how frigging brown I am. For all I know, I've got black blood in me, somewhere on my family tree. Just like you must have some Hun in your ancestry. Maybe that's what makes you so mean, sometimes. Not that I'm complaining."

"Um, point taken. We're both probably mongrels, to some extent or other. Anyway, about my buddy — you don't have to take my word for it. I have a photo of Officer Patterson here on my phone. Here, let me send it to you."

Soon Cordero was looking at the photo, which showed Emeric and his fellow cop, both in uniform, standing very close together, grinning at the camera. Emeric's arm was casually draped around the black man's broad shoulders. The guy named Patterson was quite a stud — a huge, muscular young man whose pecs and biceps threatened to split the seams of his tight-fitting uniform shirt. He was handsome, and he and Emeric made a sexy salt-and-pepper couple.

"You've been nailing *that,* and you still manage to find time for me?" Cordero asked. "I'm flattered."

Emeric chuckled. "I like variety."

"Me, too. Wait a minute. If you and this cop buddy of yours are both tops, then what do the two of you do in bed?"

Emeric laughed again. "Use your imagination," he suggested. "The roles aren't necessarily all that rigid."

"Okay, consider it *sold, to the horny Puerto Rican guy.* I'll see you two on Friday, when you get off work," Cordero told him.

Between then and Friday, needless to say, Cordero was in an agony of erotic expectation. Cock — hard, hot cop cock — was all he could think about. *God, what a slut I am!* He forced himself not to masturbate. He wanted to save up his spunk, so he could expend it in the company of the two sexy police officers. Staying celibate like that was a struggle for him, but he persevered.

There was no doubt about it. He had a bad case of cop fever! But he didn't want to be cured.

When the two cops showed up at his place on Friday evening, Cordero was a bit disappointed to see that they weren't wearing their uniforms. They'd changed into casual civilian clothes — in which, admittedly, they looked good.

And he wasn't disappointed by Officer Patterson. Not at all! He'd looked good in that photo. In person, he was even better. Damn, he was a fine-looking man!

If a gay man tried to come up, in his imagination, with a stereotypical, porno image of a big, black stud, a buck who was born to fuck, then Patterson would've filled the bill, more than satisfactorily. God, Cordero was hot for him from the moment he first set eyes on him. He was surprised he didn't start drooling, panting, and sniffing, like a dog in heat.

His lustful interest wasn't lost on Emeric, the son of a bitch! He seemed amused by Cordero's barely disguised desire for his buddy.

Emeric made the introductions. "Cordero, this is Officer Bruce Patterson."

"Pleased to meet you, sir," Cordero said, as he and Patterson shook hands.

"Patterson, as in Irish," the black cop joked. "Black Irish."

Emeric chortled. "You know, I must've heard that one a hundred times, but it's still as funny as it was the first time." He grinned. "Not! Like I keep telling you, Bruce. Don't quit your day job."

Bruce also smiled. "We've got at least three of the races represented here. White, brown, black. All we need is a Gaysian, and we'd have ourselves a queer United Nations."

"I'm color blind, myself," Emeric said. "All I care about is whether a man has his equipment in good functioning order."

Cordero offered his guests their choice of drinks. The three men were sitting there, cheerfully boozing, when Cordero saw Emeric give Bruce a sly, searching, sidelong glance.

"So, Bruce," Emeric asked, "what do you think of my boy Cordero?"

"He's a hot dude, bro," Bruce replied, smiling at Cordero. "I wouldn't mind seeing him without the clothes, though."

"Easy enough to arrange. Stand up, Cordero," Emeric urged him.

Cordero rose. Moving toward him, Emeric kissed him on the lips, and as usual, Cordero thrilled to the sensation of having such a sexy guy's tongue sliding deep into his mouth. Emeric unbuttoned Cordero's shirt down the front and pulled it wide open with his hands, and then he worked it down over Cordero's shoulders and biceps to bare his torso completely. He ran his fingers over Cordero's chest while Cordero kissed him back with fervor, groping for his fuck buddy's body.

Emeric was undressing him, quite dexterously. Cordero just let him do it, rather enjoying the way the guy manhandled him, and eager to experience sex with both of the hot cops at once. His shirt and pants were soon gone, and he was nude except for his boxer shorts.

Cordero glanced, questioningly, at Bruce, whose dark brooding eyes bored into his, even as he nodded in reassurance. He broke their eye contact and scrutinized Cordero from head to foot. His ironic detachment melted into an expression of pure, raw lust, which inflamed Cordero even more than Emeric's hand — which Emeric had unceremoniously shoved down inside his boxers. Emeric began to grope Cordero, roughly manipulating his hard-on. With one hand, he grasped Cordero's dick and pushed it out into the open, through his fly. Still gripping the shaft, he placed the palm of his other hand over the glans, rubbing it.

Cordero's flesh now burned to experience Bruce's touch, as well. Cordero wanted to submit to both police officers, to obey them, to be their bitch!

"I think we'd better go into the bedroom," he pleaded, pulling away from Emeric and tucking his erection back inside his boxers in a gesture of modesty which was quite superfluous, given the circumstances.

"Sure," Emeric said.

"I need to take a leak, first," Bruce told them.

"The bathroom's that way." Emeric indicated the direction with a gesture.

Emeric led the way to Cordero's bedroom, his body swaying as he walked with an unmistakably sexual provocation.

It was dark and cool in the room. Cordero shed his shorts, and then he quickly got onto the mattress and sat up against the headboard of the bed. He felt himself trembling with excitement and anticipation.

Undressing, Emeric paused, perhaps for dramatic effect, before he peeled down his own undershorts, taking his time. Cordero guessed that the man knew that Cordero was admiring him, and that he was enjoying Cordero's reaction as he bared his magnificently proportioned body and offered it for his inspection—and his approval. When Emeric was naked, his erection jutted out from the blond-furred base of his groin. He slithered onto the bed beside Cordero and put his warm hand on Cordero's upper thigh, his fingertips nudging his ball sac.

"Ready to take care of *two* cops?" he asked Cordero, in an undertone. "Think you can handle it? That you're man enough?"

"Hell, yes! It's all I've been able to think about, ever since you suggested this," Cordero confessed. "What does Bruce like to do in bed?" he inquired, also keeping his voice low.

"You'll soon find out. Just about everything, though. Don't be shy about telling him what you want. Anything you can come up with — the odds are, he'll do it," Emeric promised, with a sultry laugh. "We did agree to go easy on you, at least at first. You can be the one to jack it up, if you want."

Bruce came into the bedroom, as casually as though the three of them had retired there to sleep, instead of to suck and fuck. For one sinking moment, Cordero wondered if perhaps the good-looking black cop didn't find him particularly attractive — maybe he wasn't Bruce's type, and he was just going through with the threesome to humor Emeric.

But then Bruce began to strip, as unselfconsciously as though he was alone in the room, and Cordero's heart pounded when he stared at the man's superb body. Interestingly, he didn't undress all the way. He had on a matching set of underwear consisting of snug-fitting briefs and a tank top, both made from a soft, thin white cotton fabric. The material covered him without concealing anything, and Cordero found the contrast between his dark skin and the white undergarments extremely erotic.

The underpants appeared to be stuffed with his stiff cock, which lay tucked up toward Bruce's navel like an enormous brown sausage. His balls appeared to be the size and shape of two eggs, and a tangle of black pubic hair protruded from under the top edge of the elastic waistband of the briefs. The tank top was stretched taut across his heavy chest, his nipples visible through the thin fabric, his pecs coated with a soft pelt of silky dark hair.

Bruce seated himself comfortably in a chair which Cordero kept in his bedroom, near the foot of his bed, disappointing Cordero's expectation that the cop would strip out of his underwear and join Emeric and him on the bed. Spreading his muscular bare legs to give Cordero an even better view of his packed briefs, Bruce watched his fellow police officer and his young sub, with a look of nonchalance on his handsome face.

"To start off with, I want to watch," Bruce explained.

Cordero was a bit piqued by his insouciance. But then, suddenly, he was excited by the idea of performing in front of him, of putting on a shameless sex show with Emeric, which he was confident would turn on the other sexy cop. When Emeric embraced him, Cordero responded eagerly, aroused as always by the man's masculine bulk and hard muscularity. He caressed Emeric's firm buttocks, his stomach, and thighs. They kissed again and again, their tongues darting into each other's mouths.

The two naked men tumbled down onto Cordero's bed in a wanton displayed of interlocking limbs. From the corner of his eyes, Cordero glanced at Bruce. He shifted in his seat and rubbed his hand over the growing bulge in those enticing white briefs of his. Cordero suspected he was getting off on watching him and Emeric. But, Cordero flattered himself by imagining Bruce was no doubt also looking forward to enjoying Cordero's body himself. All in good time!

Emeric was sucking Cordero's dick with his customary efficiency and enthusiasm. Very few of Cordero's previous sex partners could rival his cop fuck buddy when it came to delivering a blow job. Cordero felt his semen stirring deep within his pelvis—in his balls—in the core of his tingling, overexcited, mouth-loved cock. The other guy's soft, wet lips and his insidious, tireless tongue teased Cordero's tool to the verge of ejaculation more rapidly that he had ever thought possible.

Although Cordero had instinctively thrust his head between Emeric's hard-muscled thighs, he couldn't help hesitating for a moment before starting to blow him in return. He was afraid that going down on Emeric would distract him from the incredible sensations which being blown himself were giving him. That was always a potential hazard during a sixty-nine, as exciting as the act could be.

But even while Cordero stared—torn between desire and anxiety—at Emeric's blond-furred groin area and his hard, throbbing dick, he felt the first shock of ejaculation rocketing through his own body. Cordero forgot all about anything else as he came, violently, inside the cop's greedily slurping mouth!

"Oh, shit, I'm coming!" he announced. "I'm blowing my fucking wad! In your mouth, cop—yeah, take it in your mouth! Swallow that cum!"

Cordero raked the sheets with his fingers, tossing his legs high into the air, his ass cheeks tensing, his mouth open, while cries and whimpers of stunned fulfillment burst from his lips, and his cum flooded the sucking stud's throat again and again.

Sweat bedewed his thrashing body. Emeric used his weight to hold him down on the bed. Cordero shot and shot, while the cop's tongue and teeth and lips worked on his exploding prick nonstop, teasing it, tormenting him, satisfying him as he had rarely been drained by an act of oral sex before.

With a final cry of passion, Cordero took the plunge into depravity. He seized Emeric's beautiful firm buttocks to hold his pelvis steady, and he pressed his face against the man's crotch. Cordero slid his tongue over the cop's hairy balls, licking them, before he opened his mouth wide and he sucked both nuts deep inside it.

In Emeric's state of acute arousal, Cordero's clumsy but enthusiastic, indeed frenzied, efforts to satisfy him may have excited him more than a more experienced ball-sucker might have done. Emeric renewed his own oral exertions around Cordero's depleted prick.

They rolled around on the mussed bedclothes, with Cordero's darker complexion contrasting vividly with

Emeric's pale skin. They writhed together, each of them employing an insatiable mouth upon the shaft of the other's thick cock, their lips glued around the knobs.

Cordero's heavy chest heaved with the effort it took him to fill his lungs with air, and his hips jerked while he worked his hard-muscled ass cheeks in a deliberate attempt to excite the two police officers—but especially Bruce—by letting him compare Cordero's solidly muscled masculine charms to his fellow cop's equally impressive physique.

And Cordero succeeded, apparently. If his audience of one wasn't applauding, it was only because Bruce's hands were otherwise occupied at the moment!

Bruce had quickly lost his studied cool as the lewd gay spectacle the other two men were presenting unfolded before his eyes. He grunted with vicarious satisfaction, mingled perhaps with envy, when Cordero came in Emeric's hot, sucking mouth, and then he sank back in his chair, panting for breath and sweating despite the comfortable temperature of the bedroom and his own near-nudity.

Bruce's cock had sprung to full erection and the thin cotton fabric of his underwear threatened to burst at any moment if the pressure wasn't relieved. So Cordero wasn't surprised when he saw the big black cop shove the elastic waistband of his briefs down, far enough to let his cock and balls pop out from their confinement.

What a dick! Uncut, it had a large, round bulbous glans, attached to an abnormally thick shaft, the latter adorned with veins which stood out in high relief.

"Yeah, suck those cocks, you bastards," Bruce urged them, the tense, salacious edge in his voice only exciting the two guys on the bed more while they scaled the heights of man-to-man ecstasy in each other's embrace, their mouths pumping up and down on each other's creaming cocks, their hands fondling balls and buttocks and pecs. Hot sweat lubricated their enmeshed flesh. "Suck those cocks! Suck them *off!* Swallow down that fucking cum!"

Bruce spat into the palm of his right hand, which he closed tightly around his cockshaft. Cordero heard him grunting with satisfaction as he made the first instinctive masturbating motions, his fist sliding up to the crown of his solid hard-on, stretching the foreskin over the glans — and then returning to the base of the thick dark dick with a rapid milking motion. Cordero could empathize with him. He was sure he knew just what Bruce was experiencing, based on his own innumerable jack-off sessions. The action of the cop's fist on his cock was surely sending hot waves of pleasure rippling through his perineum muscle and his balls. Cordero was willing to bet that his puckered, constricting ass hole was flexing in sync with the rhythm of his hand motions, too!

"Ah, fuck!" Bruce gasped, only half-aloud, while he added the delights of jerking off to the visual thrill of observing Emeric and Cordero going down on each other on the bed, only a yard or so away from where he sat in his chair.

After long, exciting minutes, all three of the participants in this private drama of erotic excess could take no more without proceeding to still wilder — and ultimately even more satisfying — activities. Cordero broke away from Emeric with a gasp, flinging himself over the bed at full length, while the cop refused to relinquish his grip on his bedmate's hips, sucking on his sensitive prick nonstop.

"Goddamn it, Emeric! You fucker! Stop it. I'm going to come — *again* — if you keep that up," Cordero warned him. "Christ! It's almost too much. *Too* good!" His cock felt as though it had been dipped in liquid fire. The cop's hot, skilled cocksucking mouth was driving him wild. "Yeah, go on," Cordero urged him, contradicting himself. "Keep your mouth and tongue going on me. Suck that cock, cop! I *want* to shoot again! I'm almost there. Oh, Emeric! Suck my dick, suck it hard! Make it come!" Mad with lust, Cordero stared at Bruce. "What's the matter, dude?" Cordero taunted him. "Are you all talk and no action? Are you just going to sit there and watch, all night? Come on, get your ass over here. I want your cock."

Smirking, Bruce roused himself from his voyeuristic and masturbatory reverie.

"Be careful what you wish for," he advised.

"Bring it on!" Cordero insisted.

The sexy sight of Cordero squirming on the bed like that, stark naked, his hair disheveled and stray locks of it strewn across his hot flushed face—his mouth wide open, spouting obscenities as he begged Emeric to finish sucking him off— his strong thighs quivering with tension while the handsome cop knelt between them and massaged his meat with his mouth, sucking him, with greedy, shameless slurping noises and deep gulps for breath—it was all apparently too much for Bruce.

He no doubt could feel his prick pulsating within his fist as his own climax approached, and he had no intention of letting his cum go to waste—not when his fellow cop and his sub were both within easy reach, and they were surely more than willing to help out a third horny guy.

Clumsily, Bruce got to his feet and stepped out of his underbriefs. Then, staggering toward the bed, he pulled the tank top over his head. Nude, he knelt on the edge of the mattress, his hard-on once again grasped in his fist, his muscular dark body glowing with sweat and a flush of intense sexual heat.

He seized a handful of Cordero's mussed hair and pulled his head down to his crotch, forcing Cordero to twist his upper body so that he could blow him at the proper angle while Emeric's uninterrupted oral ministrations brought him off.

"Suck my black dick, you hot fucking Puerto Rican motherfucker," Bruce grunted. "Come on, open your mouth! Get it down on that thing!"

Eagerly, Cordero wet his dry lips with his tongue and closed them firmly around the head of Bruce's throbbing dick. He sucked more than half of that immense organ straight into his mouth, and the black stud cop nearly exploded on the spot.

"That's right," Bruce gasped. "Suck it, punk, and you'd better suck it good. Maybe Emeric lets you get away with a lot of crap. Not me! I'm going to own your ass."

At the risk of seeming racist and promulgating stereotypes, Cordero really got off on sucking the cop's big, black cock. But the fact was, Bruce *was* hung heavy, a match for Emeric, who was as large as any guy he'd ever blown, and as a result Cordero had to strain his jaws apart to get his mouth open wide enough to accommodate him. Then, too, Cordero was so excited by what Emeric's tongue was doing to him, by the tremendous, delayed ejaculation he could feel building up in his swollen balls, that it was difficult for him to control his breathing and take Bruce's heroically proportioned cock easily down into his throat.

Cordero gagged and choked as he struggled manfully to get that huge hard-on into the proper position to deep-throat it, but he was determined to blow Bruce and to blow him well, so he ignored his momentary discomfort.

The rest of Bruce's prick disappeared into his mouth and descended into his gullet inch by inch, almost making Cordero lose consciousness when all of that solid meat blocked off his breath altogether — until he managed to find a way to work it in and out of his throat, snatching quick, shallow breaths around its bulk every time he could.

Cordero felt his entire body being convulsed by a phallic explosion which made his previous orgasms seem like a feeble twitch by comparison. His cock spurted a steady stream of rich, pungent fuck fluids into Emeric's thirsty mouth, while the blond cop — gasping between sucks and gulps, his broad shoulders shaking — used his own hand to bring himself off at the same moment, fisting his dick repeatedly with hard, rough strokes until it, too, shot off in a torrent of sperm, drenching the sweaty sheets.

"Fuck, yeah! Take it — swallow it — suck me dry, take it all!" Bruce commanded. His cock jerked and trembled deep within the saliva-wetted tunnel of his cocksucker's throat. "Suck me off, Cordero — swallow it all right down, taste my hot cum. Don't take that beautiful soft cocksucking mouth of yours away from my cock until you've sucked down all of my cream. Every salty drop!"

As though, in his overheated, sexed-up condition, Cordero had any intention of doing otherwise! Even if Bruce's gushing cum choked him to death! He let out a deep, brazen grunt of passion when he felt the first slick, salty wad of the cop's thick semen filling his throat.

He left half of Bruce's prickshaft slip up out of his throat, keeping his lips tightly sealed around the head, however, so that he could taste the stud cop's spurts upon his tongue while he flicked it over the spitting glans of the penis, rubbing it sensuously.

Cordero held his breath and used his mouth on Bruce's frenulum, working his cum-slippery lips rapidly to and fro on the upper part of that thick column of stiff flesh to increase the intensity of Bruce's orgasm. The black man came and came, flooding his mouth and throat with the warm, trickling jets of his potent male seed.

Sweat broke out all over Cordero's shivering body while Bruce pumped the last spurts of his sex sauce between his milking lips. At last, Cordero had to open his mouth wider, to grab a quick, deep breath. Bruce's dick slipped out of his oral grip and struck his cheek, splattering his face with the last few drops of his sticky spunk.

With a moan, Cordero stuck out his tongue to lick clean the softening cock which now swung, depleted, in front of Bruce's relaxed, emptied balls. The musky odor of a man's crotch after sex filled his nostrils when Cordero sagged down on the bed, clinging to the black cop's muscular thighs for support.

Cordero sensed that Emeric was sliding alongside him, kissing his pecs and his nips, using his hand where his tongue had been only moments before, arousing Cordero's prick yet again from the languor which inevitably followed a debilitating orgasm.

Emeric bent down, took Cordero's face between his hands, and, raising it, he kissed him on the mouth. His tongue explored the warm interior of Cordero's panting mouth, tasting the cum which his cop buddy had just shot into it.

Then Emeric broke their kiss and laughed, his brooding, sensual eyes — now warm and relaxed from sex — only inches from Cordero's own orgasm-dazed ones. Cordero buried his face in the man's sweaty chest, and he let Emeric stroke his upper body with both of his hands while they clung together.

During their embrace, Bruce continued to masturbate Cordero, while his breath came and went in labored gasps, his body tensing from time to time in involuntary response to this relentless stimulation.

"Still hard, huh, kid? Good! Fuck me," Bruce groaned, reaching for the tube of lubricant beside the bed, squeezing a glob of it onto his fingers, and plunging them shamelessly between his buttocks, massaging the lube into his puckered ass hole. "Keep it hard and fuck my cop ass with it, man!"

"Jesus, guys. I've already come, real hard," Cordero pointed out. "Don't know if I can shoot off again. Not so soon, anyway."

"Shit!" Bruce scoffed. "At your age, a guy can come over and over again. Just shove it up my ass. I bet my hole will keep you hard inside me, even if you can't come."

The guy wasn't exactly talking like a top, but Cordero found the prospect of screwing him highly arousing.

"You're going to love plugging my buddy's tight little butt," Emeric promised Cordero, while he toyed with Cordero's swollen, inflamed nips. "And I'm going to love watching it!"

"Yeah?" Bruce retorted. "Well, while you're watching, you can shove *your* cock in my mouth," he urged his fellow police officer. "Fuck my face while Cordero fucks my ass. Give it to me from both ends, guys!"

As all three of them quickly rearranged their bodies so that Bruce could sandwich himself between Emeric and Cordero, Cordero wondered if they were ever going to stop sucking and fucking. He certainly hoped not!

CHAPTER TEN: A LEATHER ORGY

"I'm glad you like Bruce," Emeric remarked to Cordero, after one of their sex sessions. "He's just about my best friend, on the force."

"Bruce? Not Frank?" Cordero asked. Frank, also known as Donut Boy, was Emeric's partner.

"Partners can work together well without necessarily being friends. In fact, maybe a bit of distance enhances the working relationship. It's like having a really good fuck buddy. Too much intimacy outside of the bedroom can lower the temperature of the sex. I prefer mine hot."

"Then that's why —"

"Why what?" Emeric demanded when Cordero hesitated.

"Nothing."

"No, tell me."

"You do seem to have a thing about not letting yourself get too close to a guy, outside of the bedroom, as you say."

To Cordero's relief, Emeric didn't seem offended.

"Maybe," he admitted. "I'll work on it, okay? In fact, I was about to suggest you and I have a night out together."

Cordero smiled. "A date?"

"Well, sort of a date. We'd be socializing, certainly, with a bunch of other guys. Let me run it by you. Do you know a rich guy named Eliot?" Emeric asked Cordero.

"I don't know *any* rich guys," Cordero replied. "If I did, I'd suck up to him and try to make him my sugar daddy. Do you?"

Emeric grunted. "This dude is just an acquaintance of

mine. He's got plenty of money to throw around, and he doesn't hesitate to spend it on fun and games. I have to say that much for him. He owns a building downtown, among his other properties, and once a month or so he has a group sex party there."

"I've never been to a real sex party. Guess I don't have to ask whether *you* have."

"Variety's always nice."

"Huh," Cordero grunted, ambiguously.

"A good crowd always shows up for these gangbangs. Even guys from out of town. Anyway, I'm invited to the next one. So is Bruce. It's on Saturday night, the fifth. Want to come?"

"I'm not invited."

"You'll be welcome. Bringing a plus-one is encouraged, as long as he's hot."

"What goes on at this sort of thing?"

"Just about anything. Don't worry. Bruce and I'll be there to protect you from the predatory homosexuals. If anybody molests you without your permission, we'll bust him. Just make sure you make it clear when you're being molested *with* your consent, so we'll know the difference."

"Oh, in *that* case," Cordero said, imitating Emeric's sarcasm. "Then, definitely, I'll come."

"It's bareback optional," Emeric informed Cordero. "So BYOR."

"BYOR?"

"Bring Your Own Rubbers."

"Oh. Got it."

"Also any leather gear and favorite toys that you might want to use."

In the course of a subsequent conversation, Emeric told Cordero more about what he could expect.

The building which the mysterious host, Eliot, owned was

a warehouse. The property had been in his family for years. He leased most of the space out, to a number of companies, for them to use as storage.

"But the top floor," Emeric explained. "That, Eliot has reserved for his own use. It's very private, especially at night, because nobody works on the other floors except during the daytime. He even has the elevator rigged so that you can only access the top floor with a key."

"And he uses this top floor as—" Cordero asked.

"His playroom," Emeric said. "It's quite a nice setup, I must say. Lots of room to spread out. There's equipment. Restraints, that sort of thing. There's a core group of regulars who usually show up, but Eliot's always looking to recruit new talent. This next get-together on Saturday evening will start around ten, and it'll go on for as long as the guests want to, through Sunday morning. There's nothing for you to be nervous about. You'll fit right in."

"I'd like to fit in. It sounds like fun."

It *did* sound like fun, although during the few days before Saturday rolled around, Cordero pondered the implications of this upcoming *date* with Emeric.

Theirs was a sexual relationship. Emeric had made it perfectly clear that both of them were free to hook up with other guys. In fact, Emeric seemed to encourage it. First Bruce, and now this sex party!

But Emeric had also said he was willing to work on his intimacy issues.

Screwing around with a bunch of strangers — that doesn't sound like a way for us to get closer to each other. Maybe I ought to start standing up to Emeric, a little. Sticking up for myself, not always being his doormat.

But I don't want to risk scaring him off. I started fucking around with him on his terms. A little late to try to renegotiate the rules now.

Damn it, a guy just can't seem to win! For now, I guess my best bet is just to go with the flow. If Emeric wants to go to an orgy, then I'll go there with him. If he wants me to be a whore, then I'll act like a whore. Whatever!

Yeah, whatever it takes to hold on to him. I don't want to lose him.

Emeric, Bruce, and Cordero drove to the warehouse together, in one car, on Saturday night.

Eliot had one muscular young man in leather gear manning the elevator, using the key to take guests up to the top floor. There, an even larger hulk was on duty, a giant of a man, overly muscular and rather dumb-looking. He seemed to be a combination greeter and bouncer. After looking the trio of new arrivals over, he nodded, as though giving his tacit approval and permission for them to join the party.

There didn't seem to be an official guest list. If a guy looked hot, he was welcome, and he was allowed in.

The top floor of the building was essentially a loft space, one vast open area, although some parts of it were divided by internal walls which didn't reach all the way to the ceiling. The lights were turned down low, creating an intimate, if also somewhat gloomy and even slightly sinister, ambience.

Cordero was surprised to see at least three dozen men milling about in the large open space. It might have been a Saturday night at one of the city's gay bars — in fact, many of the bars' regular customers appeared to have deserted the drinking establishments for one evening, in order to attend this private party.

Long folding tables held food and booze. The guests wore leather and denim, with various parts of their bodies exposed. Many were already nude, totally, or except for their boots.

"Oh, here comes our host now," Bruce remarked.

Cordero received a shock. The smiling man who approached and greeted them looked familiar to Cordero, who recognized him after a moment. The delay was caused by the man's gaudy, ostentatious attire, which was distracting. He wore supple, high-grade black leather trousers, vest, and jacket, all obviously custom-made and at great cost, from head to foot. The elaborate outfit was accessorized with brightly polished chrome chains, dangling everywhere, rattling together whenever the man moved.

The real giveaways, so far as Cordero was concerned, were the guy's tight, hard-muscled little body, his expensive haircut, his neatly trimmed mustache, and the large-carat, twinkling diamond studs set in his pierced earlobes. To say nothing of the fact that he was costumed as though he'd just come from modeling for a BDSM fashion shoot. His alert, open, eager, decidedly sexual facial expression provided further proof of his identity.

Apparently, Cordero *did* know at least one rich man, at least on the basis of a casual, fleeting barroom acquaintance. Eliot was none other than the *clone* who'd pawed Cordero drunkenly in the bar on the night Cordero had met Emeric!

Emeric introduced Cordero to Eliot.

"We've met," Cordero said.

That statement obviously piqued Emeric's interest, although he said nothing.

"Have we?" Eliot asked, looking at Cordero quizzically.

"Ah, yes, we met in one of the bars one night," Cordero explained.

"Oh, that explains it. I meet so many men in bars! You'd think I'd remember a good-looking number like you, though. Sorry, but I don't."

"Oh, that's okay. It was a brief encounter."

"We didn't go home together?"

"No."

"God, I must be slipping!" Eliot exclaimed, in mock horror. "Well, now that you're here, I'm glad you could make it, gentlemen." Eliot purred. "It's clothing optional, as you see.

There's a clothes check over there. That boy will put your things in a numbered bin and give you a ticket, on a rubber band you can put around your wrist or your ankle. And he'll stand guard over your things. Strip down, if you want to, and then have something to eat and drink."

That was exactly what the trio did. They, too, shed most of their garments, retaining only their boots and few accessories. They helped themselves to the food and liquor. Eliot, Cordero had to admit, was a conscientious and generous host, who sure knew how to throw a party and make his guests feel at home. He'd provided food and booze, both of excellent quantity and quality.

The evening was full of surprises for Cordero. He found himself standing at the buffet table next to none other than Riley! His friend, the mechanic, had undressed, retaining only his boots and his black leather motorcycle jacket, which was open in front to expose his torso piercings. Below the jacket, his junk and his bare butt hung out, for all to view—quite a sight.

"Well, look who's showed up," Riley remarked, grinning. "My favorite college jock."

"You know Eliot?" Cordero asked.

"Sure. I work on his cars. He'd got a Cadillac and a Jaguar. Man, that Jag is a sweet set of wheels," Riley declared, with a sigh. "And I never miss one of his parties. About time you showed up at one."

"Nobody invited me—or even told me about them—until now."

Riley laughed. "Maybe we were worried about having too many of you fresh-faced, wholesome college boys hang out with us degenerates. If word got around to the campus, we could be accused of corrupting you."

"You must know Bruce and Emeric, then." Cordero indicated the police officers, who stood out of earshot at the moment, but who acknowledged Riley's presence with nods and smiles.

"The hot cops? Hell, yeah. The three of us had a good time together at the last party."

"I bet." Cordero felt a bit sullen, not to mention jealous and left out. Everybody in town seemed to have been merrily orgying away except for him!

"This is a sweet setup. I'd like to move in here," Riley joked, as he munched on a sandwich and guzzled a cold beer taken from a bucket of ice.

"Yeah," Cordero agreed, as he, too, ate and drank. "I wonder if Eliot could use a houseboy? I'd apply for the job."

"Imagine being able to afford to keep a place like this, just for sex. To have the food catered. And to be able to hire guys to run the elevator, guard the door, and do the clothes check. At other sex parties, they put out a jar or a coffee can, you know, to toss contributions in, to help pay for the food and booze. Not Eliot. He won't take our money. He'd loaded enough to not give a shit about such things." Riley snickered. "Hell, the guy probably keeps a wad of cash in his john at home and uses it for toilet paper!"

"Then next time, I hope I'm invited to his house, so I can help myself to some of *that* brand of toilet paper," Cordero joked. "Been to a lot of sex parties, have you?"

"Not enough."

Having had a chance to become acclimated, Cordero observed what was going on around him.

An atmosphere of hedonism, of unrestrained sexual openness and freedom, seemed to prevail in the warehouse's loft space.

Some items of furniture—couches, armchairs, coffee, and end tables—were arranged in various configurations, throughout the big room. The pieces all looked old and used, second-hand, well broken in, but the seats were comfortable. Here and there, on the floor, were placed mattresses, each of which was equipped with a fitted bottom sheet. These were the improvised beds upon which the guests were welcome to lie while they sucked and fucked.

The event had been advertised as a bareback sex party, and Emeric had mentioned Bring Your Own Rubbers, but condoms were in fact supplied, in clear plastic bowls, for those who wanted them. Lubricants and stacks of towels were placed next to the mattresses, as well.

The lighting was dim, enhancing the intimate, seductive mood. Large areas of the floor space were lost in shadows.

"This is like one of the orgy rooms in a bathhouse," Bruce commented to Riley, after moving to greet him. "One big orgy room."

"Yeah," Riley agreed.

Emeric had also come to say hello to Riley. But then Emeric turned to Cordero.

"If I can trust you on your own—then I'm going to circulate," Emeric said.

"Yeah, me, too," Bruce agreed. "Yell if you need backup," he advised Cordero. "Just call out *Code Sixty-Nine*, especially if you need a fresh cock or two," he joked.

He, Emeric, and Riley wandered off, exploring, circulating among the guests.

Eliot sought out Cordero. The host had checked most of his elaborate leather garb, joining in the general near or total nudity. "Having a good time?"

"Oh, yeah."

"Shoot off yet?"

"Um, no," Cordero replied.

"Saved it for me, I hope. Come on, stud," Eliot urged. "You and I have unfinished business to attend to."

He led Cordero to one of the couches. The two men strutted

around in front of the couch for a few moments, exhibiting their virtually nude bodies and their exposed and erect sex organs to anyone who cared to glance in their direction. They embraced, kissing and caressing each other.

Several of the guests reached out with their hands, touching the two guys, fondling their muscles, grabbing their asses and their cocks and balls. Cordero and Eliot did nothing to discourage them. Men knelt and kissed and sucked their dicks, and then one guy silently urged Eliot to bend over the couch, so he could lick his ass. Holding onto the back on the couch with both of his hands, Eliot brazenly shoved his butt back into the guy's face, obviously enjoying the way his guest's tongue poked up into his ass hole and wormed around wetly inside it, while the onlookers observed the rim job and jacked off.

"That's right," one man moaned. "Suck that butch ass hole. Oh, get your fucking tongue in that hole, as far as you can. Get it wet. Get it warmed up for me. I'm next. I want to suck that ass, too!"

Meanwhile, Cordero wasn't idle. A second man was rimming him. That ass-hungry man dug his fingers into Cordero's glutes as Cordero parted his butt cheeks and he allowed the guy to stab his tongue deep into his rectum.

"Uh, yeah, eat that ass," Cordero gasped. "Oh, your tongue feels good in my hole, dude!"

After the rimming, Cordero and Eliot lay down side by side on the couch, where they played with each other's pricks. Then Cordero grabbed his host in a bear hug, putting his arm behind his neck, and he pushed Eliot's face down to his chest. Eliot closed his lips around Cordero's left nipple, sucking hard on the stiffened flesh, and nibbling at it with his teeth. He slid his mouth across Cordero's pecs to attack the right nipple, too.

Next, Eliot slid his lips down Cordero's torso, to his navel, which he tickled with the tip of his tongue, and to his abs, which he kissed and licked. Moving his mouth down still lower, he lapped at the dark pubic bush above the root of Cordero's erection.

"Oh, go ahead, Eliot, suck that big Puerto Rican cock," one of the guests moaned.

That was just what Eliot seemed to have every intention of doing. He swallowed Cordero's prick, and he began to deep-throat it. Grunting, Cordero twisted his body around on the couch cushions until he and Eliot lay in a sixty-nine position. Opening his mouth, Cordero took the other man's meaty dick inside it.

"Shit," another man exclaimed, in awe. "Look at those guys suck! What a couple of hot bodies! What a pair of big cocks!"

Oblivious to the presence of the other men in the room, Eliot and Cordero pumped their mouths vigorously, feeding on each other's cocks. Several guys stood near them and fondled themselves while they watched the hot sixty-nine action.

Cordero interrupted their reciprocal sucking. "Don't come yet, dude," he begged Eliot. "You want to fuck me, don't you? Sure you do. Shove it up my ass."

"*You're* a bottom?" Eliot inquired, incredulously.

"Yeah. Tonight I am, for sure. I want to get fucked. Oh, shit—you're a bottom, too, aren't you?" Cordero recalled Eliot's drunken behavior in the bar. As though in a flashback, Cordero vividly remembered the man saying, *I'd like to take you home with me and let you do dirty things to me. You can order me around and make me service you, like your submissive little bitch. Oh, I like it when a man gets rough with me.*

Now, Cordero was sorry he hadn't taken the man up on his offer!

"That's all right," Eliot assured him. "I like it either way. I'll screw you, stud."

"Oh, thank God," Cordero moaned. "Somebody hand me some lube, okay, guys?"

"And a rubber, too?" Eliot suggested. "Or do you want it raw? Bareback?"

"No, better play safe."

A man took a plastic pump bottle of lube from beside one of the mattresses on the floor, handing it to Eliot, who didn't utilize it right away. First, Eliot rimmed Cordero, in a way which confirmed he knew how to take care of his guests and show them a good time. He thrust his tongue through Cordero's pucker and up inside his ass, as far as could. Cordero moaned with delight, and he pushed his butt firmly against Eliot's mouth.

The guests watched with rapt attention, as Eliot darted his agile tongue in and out of Cordero's heated and agitated anus.

"Hell, yeah," Cordero panted. "Get it in there, man. All the way in. Lick and suck that ass. But then, goddamn you, you'd better fuck it, and you'd better fuck it good and hard."

The same anonymous onlooker, moving in closer to observe the action, obligingly put a condom in Eliot's hand. Ripping open the foil packet, Eliot extracted the rubber and rolled it down over his cock, sheathing his erection in the latex. Demonstrating an admirable skill for multitasking, Eliot managed this without once taking his face out from between Cordero's buttocks or interrupting his licking of his ass. Soon, though, Eliot lubricated his gloved cock and Cordero's ass. Then, with Cordero on his knees on the couch and Eliot behind him, Eliot's thick prick slid deeply into Cordero's willing and receptive ass.

"Fuck, you bastard, fuck," Cordero urged, tightening his sphincter and his internal muscles to grip and massage his fucker's cock, and ensure him a hot, hard ride.

With each thrust Eliot made, his balls banged against Cordero's solid butt cheeks. Eliot wrapped his arms around his waist, and he kissed him on his sweaty back, between his shoulder blades, while he pounded his manhood into Cordero's seething manhole.

"Bitch, I'm going to shoot," Eliot warned.

"Who're you calling a bitch? Just because I'm letting you top me doesn't mean that—aw, what the fuck! Who gives a damn? Top or bottom, it's all the same. Just sex. Do it. Breed me, you dirty motherfucker. Shoot that load of cum right up my butt."

In his frenzy, Cordero ignored the fact that Eliot's prick was encased in the condom. If he did ejaculate while inside Cordero, Eliot's semen would be safely contained within the rubber's nipple-shaped reservoir tip.

In his imagination, though, in his lurid fantasy, Cordero almost believed he could feel his fucker's cock expand, deep inside his ass, and then, abruptly, hot jets of sperm shoot over his prostate, filling his anal tunnel.

But Eliot had a surprise in store for him.

Instead of coming inside Cordero, Eliot abruptly ripped his dick out of his cringing manhole. Yelping in protest at the sudden, unexpected evacuation of his anus, Cordero heard the snapping noise as Eliot stripped the rubber off his ready-to-erupt tool.

"Cum shot," Eliot explained, breathlessly, taking his now bare dick in his hand and stroking it. "Just like in porn."

A moment later, his sperm splattered wetly all over Cordero's back and buttocks. The onlookers moaned and howled with delight and approval when they saw Cordero being bathed in sperm.

Cordero let out a deep moan of pleasure. *Uh, shit, he's really wetting me down!*

While Eliot was still spraying onto him, Cordero ejected his own jism all over the couch cushions.

"Yeah," Cordero groaned, contentedly. "Oh, yeah."

"Hot ass," Eliot gasped.

Every man in the vast space now appeared to be engaging

in some sort of sexual activity, either solo, masturbating himself, or interacting with one or more partners. Recovering from their orgasms, Eliot and Cordero observed the action taking place all around them.

Chapter Eleven: Masters and Slaves

This was a night devoted to erotic abandon.

A hard-bodied man, naked except for boots, was strung up by his wrists. He stood in the open doorway of one of the interior partitions, with his arms raised and spread wide. Ropes tied around his wrists were looped over the top of the partition, drawn down tight, and secured by additional knots. The guy was forced to support himself on the balls of his booted feet — he couldn't lower himself enough to rest his heels on the floor.

A second man, also wearing only boots, stood behind him, smiting his back and buttocks and the backs of his thighs with a cat o' nine tails. That cat had claws, which bit into his body! Each impact of the flogger on the bound guy's vulnerable flesh made a cracking noise which resounded through the loft space, and it seemed to wrench a yelp of pain from his lips, as his body recoiled from the blows, swaying back and forth.

"Yeah, beat that slave's back and butt," one of the onlookers encouraged the flogger, with relish.

"Let's hear you beg for it, boy," the abuser said.

"Please, master! Please hit me harder — oh, punish me, sir!" the recipient of the flogging pleaded. "I'm a worthless piece of shit. Oh, please hurt me, sir!"

"Lousy, no-good bottom," the top man grumbled. "Don't know why I waste my time on you!" But he continued to lash the other man's cringing, reddened flesh.

Hotly aroused by this sight, Cordero finally tore himself away. There were other activities taking place all around him, to claim his attention and distract him.

He was intrigued by the sight of one couple in particular. One was a tall, extremely muscular black man, naked except for boots, a torso harness, and a heavy steel cock ring. The guy was every bit as handsome, as physically imposing, as Bruce Patterson. His companion was a much younger blond guy, who was completely nude, except for a restraint around his neck. The kid had a length of heavy chain fastened tightly around his neck with a padlock, and clipped to the chain was a black leather dog leash, which his burly black master held in his hand. As he walked across the room, the top man would give the leash a yank, to force the bottom to keep up with him.

At first, because the youth kept his head down, in a posture of submission, Cordero couldn't see his face clearly. He could tell, though, that the guy, who was about his own age, had a good, solid, pumped-up physique, obviously the product of some quality time spent in a gym.

A fellow weightlifter. Looks hot. Wonder if he goes to my school? Could be a classmate of mine! If so, he ought to be on one of the teams.

"Fuck," Eliot, who'd reappeared, muttered. "I'd like to have one of you guys do that to *me*. Lead me around like a goddamn dog."

Emeric, who was nearby and happened to overhear him, grunted. "Be careful what you wish for. I just might take you up on that. The police department could use a mascot."

The black top yanked on the blond boy's chain. The well-built younger guy was forced to raise his chin. And then Cordero got his third, and, he fervently hoped, his final shock of the night. The naked sub was none other than Joel, the captain of the college's soccer team, to which Cordero belonged!

"Shit!" Cordero exclaimed, in disbelief.

Joel saw him and cringed. "Aw, Jesus, Tejera!" he moaned. "Whatever you do, don't tell Coach you saw me here!"

"I won't," Cordero promised, automatically. The truth

was, he wouldn't have been surprised if the soccer coach was the next unexpected guest whom he'd encounter at the sex party!

The black master gave another vicious tug on the chain. "No talking unless I give you permission to speak, puppy! Understand?"

"Yes, sir," Joel whimpered.

"I ought to take a rolled-up newspaper to your ass!" With that growled threat, the man hauled Joel away, across the floor.

Cordero needed a moment to absorb the revelation that he wasn't the only local college jock who liked to be dominated by other men. But he was beginning to feel like a mere leather novice, all over again. The world of BDSM apparently included forms of depravity he had barely glimpsed yet.

He wasn't sure whether he felt sorry for Joel, or he envied him. He suspected the latter!

He turned his attention to the festivities, going on in full swing all around him.

The guests weren't shy about amusing themselves. They milled about, eating, drinking, talking. They smoked pot, and they snorted cocaine and poppers. Practically all of them had shed more or all of their clothes, sooner or later, and they were busily engaged in various forms of sexual activity. They didn't confine themselves to the furniture, or the mattresses provided. Some men had sex while standing up, or they simply got down on the floor.

Cordero was mildly surprised to see Bruce and Emeric sharing a joint.

"Not going to bust me, are you, officers?" a man asked them, as he, too, lit up.

"Nope," Bruce assured him. "We're off duty. Although we could be persuaded to make some unofficial *arrests*, if anybody wants to play cops and robbers."

"Will I get interrogated?" the man asked.

"Yeah," Emeric said.

The guy grinned. "Then count me in! I'm ready to confess. Well—maybe not until I've been slapped around a little, first."

The three men moved off, no doubt in search of a comparatively private spot in which to play out their fantasy scenario.

"I need a dick!" somebody called out, plaintively, eliciting coarse, mocking laughter from the crowd.

"Then get your mouth and your ass over here, and get busy taking care of this one," yet another guest responded.

"Oh, yeah," still another man cried, loudly. "Keep shoving things up my hole!" He was slumped in an armchair, with his legs raised and spread, and he was using his hands to hold his butt cheeks wide apart while another guest worked a huge rubber dildo back and forth inside his ass. "Get me loosened up, and then all you guys can fuck me, with your cocks! I'll take you all on. One after another, all night long. Come on, keep giving me cock."

Cordero's mouth and throat felt parched. Turning to go get himself another drink, he literally bumped into Riley.

"Been keeping yourself busy?" Riley inquired, after greeting Cordero with a hug and a kiss.

"Yes."

"Been keeping yourself out of trouble?"

"No."

"Good man. That's the spirit. This is why I never miss one of Eliot's sex parties. They're great, aren't they?"

"I know *I'm* having fun," Cordero agreed.

In the middle of the room, Cordero's teammate Joel, the young white boy who had been led in on a leash, was still on the floor on his hands and knees. His stern black master was behind him, slapping his ass with his hands. He continued the spanking until Joel's exposed buttocks were red. Then the black stud knelt down and pressed his huge unlubricated cock between the battered ass cheeks and deep into Joel's hole, groaning with satisfaction when he must have felt the heat of the anal flesh envelop his dick. Several of the guests stood nearby, observing the fuck with prurient curiosity.

One of these men crouched in front of the slave boy and began rubbing his stiff cock over his face.

"Tell all these men what you want from your big black master, you dirty little white whore," the black man demanded.

"A cock in my mouth, sir. And a fist, master," Joel babbled. "I want a fist up my ass!"

"Feel free to fuck his face," the black top man invited the guy who was teasing Joel by rubbing his dick in his face. "While I fist his nasty punk slave boy hole for him." Accepting the offer, the horny guest force-fed the kneeling Joel his cock, which the college lad slurped on, noisily.

Eliot, ever the accommodating host, appeared, with a jar of a lubricant labeled *Elbow Grease,* and a towel. "Looks like you can use this." He spread the towel over the floor and set the open jar down beside it. The black stud scooped up some of the slippery, creamy substance on his fingertips, and he inserted it into the hungrily cocksucking Joel's anus. Then he coated his fist and forearm with the grease, and he began finger-fucking his slave boy—first with one finger, then with two, before he added a third and a fourth. The bystanders observed the procedure with great interest, urging the black man on.

"That's it, Delvin, give it to him. That's a hungry hole, man. The boy wants that fist. Shove it all the way up his ass," one excited onlooker said.

Delvin looked up at his audience, smiling smugly, his eyes bright with lust and drugs, his bared teeth large, white, and even. He balled his hand into a fist, and he pushed it against Joel's tender-looking ass hole. Gradually, it disappeared inside. When the fist sank completely into the wide-stretched sphincter, several of the onlookers let out appreciative moans.

"This bitch may look kind of wimpy on the outside," Delvin said. "But I've taught him how to take it like a man."

"Yeah," the guy whose dick Joel was sucking agreed, gasping for breath. "You've trained him well. He really knows to suck!"

Bottles of poppers were being passed about the room, from hand to hand, from nose to nose, and after Cordero snorted from one of the vials, his head began swimming from the acrid fumes. Enviously, he wished he was the one, not Joel, who was on the floor being fist-fucked by the virile black man. Moving closer to the couple, he knelt down, with his face no more than a foot away from the top man's plunging forearm.

"Please, sir, I want to watch," Cordero whispered. "I want to see it going in and out of him."

"Be my guest," Delvin invited him.

Cordero touched the man's muscular forearm, ran his fingers over it, and pushed forward on the elbow, helping Delvin shove his arm farther up Joel's vulnerable, abused ass.

Joel's lust-glazed eyes met Cordero's, and he let out a long, agonized-sounding groan.

"Permission to speak, sir?" Joel asked, gasping.

"Granted," Delvin grunted.

"Please, sir, may I suck on my buddy's cock while you fist me?"

Delvin smiled at Cordero. "Got the hots for him, do you, slave?"

"Yes, master. We're on the soccer team at school. When I see him naked in the locker room and the showers after practice, I go crazy, wanting his big fat Puerto Rican dick," Joel confessed, in a breathless rush. "I want it in my mouth. Up my ass."

This was all news to Cordero, who'd always thought that Joel was kind of a stuck-up, privileged, standoffish bitch.

"Go ahead. Blow him," Delvin deigned to say.

"Thank you, sir."

One of the bystanders took over popper duty, holding a bottle under the noses of Delvin, Joel, and Cordero in turn, in each case pinching one of their nostrils shut while they inhaled through the other, open one.

Then the same man gave Cordero a gentle push in the direction of the black top man and his slave. "Go ahead, stud," the guy urged. "Fuck that pretty blond twink in his mouth. You and Delvin can let him have it from both ends. I want to watch you big-dicked numbers perform. I want to see you use the slave boy."

Cordero got down on the floor on his knees in front of Joel and fed him his cock. Eliot, who had remained nearby, observing, moved in front of Cordero, standing beside him, and he held out his wet, saliva-covered, heavily veined prick in his hand, mutely offering it to Cordero—who slipped his mouth over the flared prickhead.

While Joel sucked Cordero, and Cordero blew Eliot at the same time, Emeric and Bruce reappeared. Both cops were perspiring profusely, and they showed every sign of having just had sex, presumably with the eager *perp* who'd volunteered to be *interrogated*. They admired the skill with which Delvin plowed Joel's ass hole with his fist.

"This is quite some hot boy you've got here, man," Bruce complimented Delvin.

"Yeah, there's nothing like a submissive white man is there, bro, when it comes to taking care of a black man's cock?" Delvin replied. "White mouth and ass—black dick and fist—they go well together." Delvin turned his attention to Cordero. "Use him," the black stud urged Cordero, who was sucking cock and being sucked simultaneously. "Fuck his throat for him, really ream it out. Don't you worry about my boy Joel. Don't spare him. He'll take anything you have to give him, and he'll beg for more."

The fist-fucking became the focal point of the party. All of the guests wanted to gather around in a circle and watch the black stud fist-fuck the young white guy. One man got down on the floor and slithered under Joel until he could suck Joel's neglected cock inside his mouth. The captain of the soccer team had a fist up his ass, a cock in his mouth, and a mouth on his own prick. He shuddered, uncontrollably, his muscular, weight-trained physique in the grip of tremors of helpless passion.

As for Cordero, he was on a sustained sexual high. He was sucking on a big cock and being sucked himself while observing Joel being blown and fist-fucked at the same time. Poppers kept circulating, and the aroma of the amyl filled the air, combined with the smell of sweat and cum. When a bottle was held under his nose, Cordero inhaled deeply, repeatedly, and gratefully, feeling warmth surge through his body and his anal defenses loosen themselves. He wanted to be fucked. Again! And he wasn't feeling at all particular about by whom!

Yet another man was squatting behind Cordero, crouching down on bent knees. This guy almost seemed telepathic, able to read the lurid thoughts which were going through Cordero's mind. Half blinded by a combination of lust and amyl, which made everything blur in front of his eyes, Cordero had no more than a limited impression of the man's face and body. But he was a man, and he had a hard-on, which was all that counted, all that Cordero cared about. Grasping hold of Cordero's pistoning hips to steady them, while Cordero fucked Joel's face and throat, and sucked Eliot's cock, the mystery man began to jab his dick into the cleft between Cordero's ass cheeks.

"That's *my* boy." Cordero heard Emeric's voice announce, in a cold, no-nonsense tone. "You don't fuck him raw unless he *wants* you to bareback him—okay?"

"Yes, sir. Whatever you say, officer." Evidently the man was aware of Emeric's occupation.

"Want to be fucked, Cordero?" Emeric asked.

With his mouth stuffed full of Eliot's cock, Cordero grunted his assent.

"Put a rubber on before you screw him," Emeric urged the man.

The guy complied. Applying a squirt of lube on top of the latex, he drove his dick between Cordero's buttocks, through his pucker, and deep into his anus.

Cordero couldn't believe his luck, couldn't believe that the intense simulation he was receiving, from a multitude of sources, was real. He was sucking cock and having his own cock sucked. He was watching Delvin fist his cocksucker, Joel, who was the last guy in the world whom Cordero would ever have suspected would want to fellate him. And to top it off, he was getting a cock shoved up his own ass, pumping away frantically back and forth inside his convulsing manhole.

Sex — so much sex — so much goddamn, crazy sex! It's almost too much, all at once. I almost can't stand it. I feel like I'm going to pass out, any minute now. Either that or I'm going to come. And come harder than I ever have before in my life, come so hard that I might just die from coming! What a way to go, though. Oh, what a way to go!

Cordero pushed his buttocks back against his fucker's groin, and he could feel his anus open up in surrender and the man's penis go in deeper inside him. Cordero moved his head back and forth over Eliot's thick cock, wishing that Eliot would come in his mouth, so that he could taste and swallow the wealthy guy's sperm—and then, having drained his host, Cordero could have another man take Eliot's place and give him a fresh dick to suck on.

Eliot, too, almost seemed to read Cordero's mind. Suddenly, his thick, muscular thighs went rigid, he grunted, and he began spewing out his load and pumping it down Cordero's hungry throat. After feeding Cordero all of his sperm, Eliot withdrew his spent dick from between his lips, and he moved away—and, sure enough, another man took his place, jamming his cock down Cordero's throat. Grateful, Cordero continued his furious sucking.

His fucker came, in his ass, but inside the condom. Stepping back, the guy eased his latex-sheathed, spent dick out of Cordero's twitching behind.

Oh, if only Emeric was in there, instead, screwing me! Indulging in the fantasy that his cop stud was plowing his butt, Cordero felt no diminishment whatsoever of his acute, tormenting desire.

The man who was lying on the floor under Joel had stopped blowing him. Instead, he now had both of Joel's balls in his mouth, and he was using his hand to masturbate Joel. After a few moments of this stimulation, Joel's overtaxed prick spurted, spontaneously, bathing the ball sucker's chest with his cum. No sooner had the man released Joel's testicles and slid out from under him, than other guys attacked *him,* licking Joel's semen off his flesh.

Cordero's lungs burned from a lack of oxygen. He slid his mouth off the anonymous cock he was sucking, and, gasping for breath, he looked over Joel's head, shoulder, back, and butt. Somebody had crawled between Delvin's massive thighs, and he was sucking the black man's cock. The lewd sight triggered Cordero's long-delayed orgasm. Grunting, Cordero reached the point of no return, and he began to shoot his load down Joel's throat. Joel held some of the semen inside his mouth without swallowing it, and when Cordero stepped away, pulling his prick out of the mouth he'd just filled, his teammate pressed his face against Cordero's.

Joel and Cordero kissed, with Cordero's cum flowing from Joel's mouth back into Cordero's, so they could both taste and swallow it. Then Cordero went back to work on the prick he'd been sucking, and he mouthed it harder and faster, hoping the man would shoot off down his throat. When he did so, Cordero opened his mouth wide, and he took every drop of the proffered semen.

Emitting a loud, hoarse shout, which echoed off the walls and ceiling of the large open space, Delvin began shooting his load down the throat of the man who was between his legs, blowing him. When he finished coming, Delvin withdrew his fist from Joel's anus, and he wiped it on the towel.

"Oh, thank you, master," Joel moaned.

"Yes, thank you, sir, for letting Joel blow me," Cordero chimed in, politely.

He wondered what being fist-fucked must be like. He speculated, skeptically, whether Joel's sphincter ring and his anal tunnel would retract back to their previous, normal dimensions, after the ordeal they'd endured. Surely, his teammate's ass had been wrecked!

But that was Joel's problem. A sex madness seemed to have taken possession of Cordero. Reckless, he felt insatiable and willing to try anything which held out even the slightest prospect of eventually affording him some sexual relief.

Cordero wasn't ready to stop yet. He wanted—he *needed*—more. Much more!

Chapter Twelve: So Many Men, Such Needy Bottoms

Cordero crawled to the middle of the floor, and several men gathered around him. They faced him, displaying their erections, stroking them. The sight of the naked bodies and the stiff cocks made Cordero quiver with lust and salivate.

"I want to be a slave," he babbled.

"Then get busy, boy," one of the men said.

Cordero began sucking cocks, sucking balls, and licking asses. He moved around on his knees, from one man to another. They clustered closer around him, eager to be serviced. While he fellated or rimmed one guy, Cordero used both of his hands to jerk two more.

Eliot reappeared, drunk and stoned, a bit unsteady on his feet, and he looked down at Cordero with a smirk on his face. "Let's find out just how many men a butch young slave boy can take care of, before he decides he'd had enough cock."

One of the other men laughed. "*Is* there such a thing as too much cock?" He stood in front of the kneeling Cordero, and he plunged his fat prick down his throat. He fucked his hard-on in and out of Cordero's mouth while the others stood around and watched.

"Yeah, fuck that sexy slave in the mouth," another guest urged the one who was using Cordero's mouth at the moment. "Give the boy your load, man."

The first man responded by groaning as he pumped a thick

succession of volleys of cum down Cordero's throat. "Take it, you cum dump," the man growled as he unloaded. Cordero swallowed repeatedly, but despite his efforts, some of the semen trickled out through the corners of his mouth, ran down over his chin, and dripped onto his pecs. A few strands of the sticky jism fell to the floor.

The guy who'd just ejaculated grabbed Cordero by his hair, roughly. "You made a mess, slave. Get down there and clean it up," he barked out orders. "With your tongue!"

Cordero pressed his lips against the hard, dirty floorboards, and he licked up the spilled semen.

"Uh, shit," one of the other guests groaned. "That's what I like to see. Total submission."

"Nothing like a well-trained punk," another guy said.

Suddenly, standing beside Cordero, looming over him, was the big guy who'd been manning the door. His body was packed with thick, hard, bulging muscles. He was completely nude.

"Give me a tongue bath," he commanded Cordero, who groveled at his feet.

Wild with lust, Cordero began to lick the man, all over his impressive body. As his mouth got near the man's huge prick, the hulking muscle man grabbed a fistful of Cordero's hair and yanked his face against his meaty male organ.

"Get your mouth on it and suck it," the brute demanded. "And don't take your mouth off it until I've come in your mouth and you've swallowed every drop of my jizz."

Sucking the cock, Cordero rubbed his tongue up and down the wet shaft. Next, he dared to disobey the guy by interrupting the blow job to suck on the man's hairy balls. The big muscle man didn't seem to mind. He pulled Cordero along with him. Parking his big, hairy butt on an armchair, he threw his huge legs up in the air, and Cordero pressed his lips against his anal pucker and tongue-fucked his hole.

Wetly, Cordero wriggled his tongue up higher, applying it to the enormous piece of meat which pulsated hotly in front of his eyes. Cordero rubbed his tongue all over the big penis. He closed his lips around the glans, and he bobbed his head rapidly up and down in the man's groin, taking his dick all the way to its base. Suddenly, the big man's body stiffened, and he began to pump his load of hot slippery sperm down Cordero's throat.

Another hard, demanding cock was shoved up Cordero's ass, without the benefit of a condom or any lube. Cordero took it, dry and raw, without any complaint, in fact rejoicing in the discomfort which the abrupt, scraping insertion coat him.

"Fuck me, oh, fuck me," Cordero babbled as the anonymous man took him anally, humping away with brutal abandon.

"Suck on this, boy, while that motherfucker pounds your ass," another man advised, offering Cordero his dick. Gratefully, Cordero swooped his mouth down on the rigid male organ. Now he was getting cock from both ends, fore and aft, his mouth and throat filled and plowed with a fury which fully matched the jackhammering he was receiving in his anus.

He took a load of cum in his mouth. He took another load of cum in his ass. The spent cocks were pulled out of his orifices. But other hot, hard erections immediately took their place, filling the oral and anal voids.

"Why, that's the kid who came in with Emeric and Bruce," a guest exclaimed, no doubt suddenly remembering when he'd seen Cordero for the first time that night. "And to think—the boy looks and acts so fucking macho, when he's not down on his knees sucking cock and taking it up his ass!" This comment elicited guffaws of laughter from the onlookers.

"Look, Bruce." Cordero heard Emeric's voice call out,

mockingly. "Our little boy's all grown up. He's taking dick like a pro. I'm so proud of him."

"Yeah," Bruce growled. "He's got all the makings of a first-class leather whore!"

"Cum dump," another one of the guests remarked. "The kid is just a cum dump!"

Emeric laughed. "And that's wrong because?"

Answer came there none, except for some further laughter in response to the police officer's witticism.

Meanwhile, Eliot seemed to be doing his damnedest to rival Cordero in sheer piggy whorishness. The host of the party had appropriated one of the mattresses on the floor. With the *Elbow Grease* at hand, he was multitasking, being fist-fucked by one man while another guy squatted over his face and *forced* Eliot to suck and tongue-fuck his ass. Other men were forming two queues — one of guests waiting patiently to fist Eliot's ass in turn, the other of guys ready to sit on his face. The owner of the building was going to have himself a busy night, entertaining his guests.

Not to be outshone by the competition, Cordero shuddered and sweated, and breathed hard and moaned, in the grip of an erotic frenzy, a sustained and insatiable arousal unlike anything he had ever previously known.

Reality and fantasy seemed to blur together, becoming one. Sex madness consumed him.

He only knew that he was in the center of a group of naked male bodies which thrashed about wildly. Anonymous hands reached out to touch and fondle him. Somebody jammed a cock into his mouth, while another man straddled Cordero and sat on top of his head, with his large balls bouncing before Cordero's dazed eyes. Cordero wished he could get the testicles in his mouth, too, alongside the first man's cock, and suck on them both at once.

Two men pressed their dicks against Clint's pecs, rubbing

them over his stiff nipples. Other guys stood near him, jerking off rapidly. They all glanced at one another, admiring the fisted pricks, trying to judge their degree of arousal so that they could all shoot off as close together as possible. Somebody lifted Cordero's legs and began fucking him up the ass, all over again. It was painful, but Cordero exulted in it. Then, raising his excitement to a still higher, dizzying level, a hot wet mouth descended around his own prick, sucking it, stimulating it, soothing it.

Cordero knew that he had found what he'd been searching for, ever since he'd first gotten involved in the leather scene. His goal was ultimate degradation during sex acts, to become a cum dump for other men. He gloried in the perversity. He wanted to be a slave—and not just to Emeric and Bruce He fantasized that the two stud cops would eventually tire of him and pass him on to their police officer buddies, a plaything to be used for their pleasure as communal property. Cordero would be the precinct whore, the cops' trusty stress reliever.

He imagined, too, Riley handing him off to his fellow bikers, during wild gangbangs like this one. That was all fine with Cordero. Any kind of sex, anywhere, anytime, with anybody!

His ass spasmed around the rapidly thrusting penis which was inserted deep inside it. The man he was sucking began to ejaculate in his mouth, sending his frothy jism down Cordero's thirsty throat. Cordero felt hot streams of cum spurting onto his pecs, wetting his pecs and nipples, and splashing onto his abs, his thighs—onto every part of his shuddering, sweat-soaked body, in fact.

He was being bathed in sperm, showered in a rainstorm of thick creamy fuck fluid. While the men who were jacking off over him continued to spray their seed down upon him, Cordero writhed about on the floor, running his hands over his cum-slathered body, wishing that he was fully immersed in it—swimming in it—drowning in a sea of sperm!

Chapter Thirteen: Learning the Ropes

Somewhat to his surprise, Cordero recovered from the sex party with no lasting ill effects.

"I shouldn't have barebacked," he told Emeric. "I got a little drunk and high."

"We'll get you on PrEP," Emeric suggested. "Then you can use a condom as an extra safeguard, or not, as the mood takes you. Meanwhile—you like threesomes, don't you?" he inquired.

"Depends on who the third guy is," Cordero replied. "I sure liked getting into that one with you and Bruce."

"Then we'll have to do it again, soon. You, me, and some other guy, not Bruce—just for the sake of variety. And I've been thinking. You ought to try topping, for a change. As part of your ongoing BDSM education."

"You mean—I get to top *you?*" Cordero asked, eagerly.

Emeric smiled. "Dream on, kid. You'll need a lot more experience before you can top a cop. We'll have to work up to that gradually. Meanwhile, being dominant can provide a submissive with a different and whole new perspective. You need to be able to empathize with the other participant in the sex act—get inside his head. It's good training."

Cordero fought back a smile of his own. Emeric was talking like a college professor, delivering a lecture to a classroom full of bored students. A smirk might not be the appropriate response to his imparting of wisdom.

"Got anybody in mind for this experiment?" Cordero asked.

"I'm thinking about your buddy Riley."

"Riley? But he's a top, isn't he?"

"He's versatile. I believe I can talk him into bottoming for us. As you know, I can be very persuasive when I want to be."

Cordero was excited by the prospect of bending Riley to his will.

Payback time, for all those occasions when he's made me his bitch! Wonder if the guy can take it the way he dishes it out?

Riley agreed to meet Emeric and Cordero, at Cordero's place.

Preparing for the threesome, Emeric gave Cordero a coil of nylon rope, purchased at a hardware store.

"Keep this beside your bed," the cop advised Cordero. "It'll come in handy. Riley's been known to like having it used on him."

Emeric also gave Cordero a cardboard box containing half a dozen bottles of liquid poppers.

"Party favors," he said, wryly. "Now we're all set to entertain our friendly mechanic."

At the day and time agreed upon, Emeric and Riley showed up at Cordero's apartment promptly.

Curious about the other two men's relationship, Cordero sat and mostly listened, while his guests chatted. Analyzing their conversation, he deduced that they'd had casual sex with each other on several occasions, but that they hadn't gotten too closely acquainted — outside of bed, that is!

Well, that's Emeric's recipe, isn't it? To keep the sex hot, as he said?

Eventually, they retired into Cordero's bedroom.

All three men got naked. Consumption of beer, followed by inhalation of poppers, had relieved them of their few inhibitions.

Riley was indeed usually a top, but he explained to Cordero that there were times when he was in the mood to assume the role of bottom. This was one of those occasions. He agreed to let the other two men tie his wrists behind his back with a piece of the rope. Riley's only proviso was that he be given a safe word. He chose *spark plug*, which seemed appropriate enough, given his occupation. Then Emeric and Cordero started to work him over — warming up his butt with strokes from one of Cordero's leather belts, before instructing him to suck their cocks and stick his tongue up their asses.

Then Cordero and Emeric edged Riley, pinching his nipples, tickling his balls, fingering his ass, and massaging his cock — taking care, though, to stop short of letting their bound victim ejaculate.

"You have to make the sub earn it," Emeric told Cordero, in his instructor mode. "You have to make him beg you for it. And then you deny him what he wants, and make him beg for it harder."

"Please, guys," Riley begged. "Have a heart. My goddamn balls ache. Look, I'm dripping cum. Please, let me shoot."

"Not yet," Emeric said.

"Not until we damn well want you to," Cordero agreed.

"You dirty, stinking motherfuckers!" Riley insulted them.

"Watch your mouth," Emeric warned. "You're nothing but a dirty man whore, here to service us," he declared, contemptuously, dismissively. "Just like at the garage, where some guy drops off his car for you to work on — and he probably gets a blow job from you, in the bargain."

"Pricks! Uh, you two dirty, lousy, stinking scumbag pricks!" Riley sputtered, defiantly.

"Fuck his face, Emeric, that ought to shut him up," Cordero suggested. "While I heat up his ass again with the belt. Bitch," he warned Riley, "you may be hot shit when you walk into a bar, with all of the customers drooling over you. But here you're just another pussy boy who needs to be put in his place."

He proceeded to warm Riley's butch butt with his belt. The leather smacked into Riley's buttock flesh and muscle with fierce impacts, each blow creating a resounding cracking noise.

Meanwhile, Emeric grabbed a fistful of Riley's long, loose red hair.

"Suck my dick, you long-haired freak," Emeric demanded. "Yeah—this mane of yours is good for one thing. A guy can hold onto it while he fucks your mouth. Open up. Swallow my goddamn cop cock. Take it right down into your throat, cocksucker!"

Gurgling, gagging, Riley blew the cop.

"What the fuck is this shit? Quit holding back. We both know you can do better than that," Emeric insisted. "Watch the teeth, punk! Keep your fucking lips curled over their edges, to cushion them. All I want to feel on my prick is your lips, not your teeth. You scrape me again, and I swear to God I'll knock your teeth down your throat and you'll be swallowing *them*. Now, *suck,* boy, *suck!* Give that big cop dick of mine a good suck!"

Inspired by watching Emeric force-feed Riley his cock, Cordero continued to apply the belt to Riley's ass. Riley was a mature, virile man, older than Cordero. It excited Cordero to be able to abuse a guy who was older than he was, and who was so masculine.

"Get that ass of his bright red and burning hot," Emeric demanded, encouraging his pupil, while he savagely fucked Riley's face. "Whip him! Belt him! Put your mark on that butt! Don't hit him in the same place twice in a row. Keep him guessing, so he never knows where he's going to feel the pain next. Warm up that whole butt."

Fueled by the amyl, all three guys were in the grip of an

erotic frenzy, as though they were suffering from a contagious fever, passing from one of them to another.

"When in doubt, use brute force," Emeric suggested, at one point in the proceedings. "That's always a good plan of attack, by God. That always gets results."

After subjecting the well-built number to some further abuse, his tormentors finally relented, to the extent of helping him come. Emeric greased his hand with the slippery sex lube which Cordero always kept handy beside his bed, and he manipulated Riley's prick—while Cordero fingered the ass hole which smoldered away between the buttocks he'd just whipped to an angry-looking, painful redness with the belt.

Tugging futilely at the rope which restrained his wrists, his tattooed arm muscles bulging from the strain, Riley shuddered and howled, as his semen escaped from his piss slit in a succession of strong wet jets.

"Aren't you going to thank us?" Emeric inquired.

"Yeah," Riley panted. "Thank you, sirs." The surly look on his face and the matching inflection in his voice suggested that he might be thinking something more along the lines of *Fuck you, you bastards!*

"He doesn't sound all that grateful to me," Cordero observed. "I'm not sure this slave boy understands who's boss, yet."

Emeric snickered. "Like the song says, my man. *Don't try to understand 'em,*" he quipped. "*Just rope an' throw an' brand em.* Go on, Cordero. Show him who's in charge."

"Yeah," Cordero growled, with a saturnine, ominous look on his face.

Riley probably experienced some apprehension, as he speculated about just how the sadistic Cordero might choose to emphasize his newfound dominance over him. Riley had already ejaculated once, to his infinite relief, but now he was experiencing a *come to Jesus* resurrection of his erection.

"Looks like you're ready to keep right on going," Cordero

commented, observing Riley's tumescence.

"Yeah," Riley gasped. "This shit is really turning me on!"

"I knew it would. Now, put my dick back in your mouth and suck on it. Get it good and hard. Then I'll give you a fuck that'll make you decide you were born to be a bottom."

Eagerly, Riley's lips wrapped themselves around Cordero's cockhead, and he began sucking on it as though the trio's previous sex acts had served only to ignite within him a burning hunger for cock. Cordero was relishing this new, still unfamiliar role of top man. The object of his domination, Riley, seemed to enjoy the feeling of submitting to another man, of being dominated and ordered around and used by him. Jerking his pelvis back and forth, Cordero fucked Riley's handsome bearded face, forcing the full length of his prick into his mouth and jabbing the glans down his saliva-lubricated throat with callous, choking force.

"Yeah, man," Emeric groaned, fully approving of what he was witnessing. "Don't let him get off easy, Cordero. Make him work for it. Train him right. Never let him forget who's in charge. He's here to satisfy his masters. His own pleasure — that's a secondary consideration."

When he was once again fully erect, Cordero pulled Riley up and pushed him onto the bed, where he arranged his long-haired, bearded prisoner's pierced and tattooed body so that Riley's bound wrists were under the small of his back and his legs were up on Cordero's shoulders, resting on either side of his neck. Next, Cordero laved Riley's ass hole with his tongue, getting it relaxed and wet with his saliva, ready for him to fuck without any need for artificial lubricant. Positioning Riley so that his butch ass was directly in front of his groin, Cordero worked his throbbing cock through his manhole and deep inside his anus. Riley let out a loud yelp of pain.

"Son of a bitch! Take it easy," Riley cried. "That's one hell of a big cock you're shoving in there, you know. Uh, you're going in deep. Damn, that thing is thick!"

"Man up and take it," Cordero advised, curtly.

"Bastard."

"Punk!"

"College faggot. Frat boy fuck!"

"Blue collar bitch."

After spitting out that insult, Cordero dug his fingertips into Riley's hips. Rearing back, he bucked his body forward, driving his dick all the way into the other guy's ass. He began to fuck his prisoner, violently, pulling his cock almost all the way out of his cringing hole, only to shove it roughly back in again.

"At least untie my hands, so I can jack off," Riley pleaded.

"No. Tough shit, dumbass. Deal with it. Suffer, bitch!"

"Then jerk it for me."

"I'm busy, boy," Cordero taunted Riley.

"Who the hell are you calling a boy? You pussy pup, you're a lot younger than me, and still wet behind your ears, you little cunt!"

"The boy seems to be doing a damn fine job of owning your ass, stud," Emeric interjected, taunting Riley.

"Yeah, because you put him up to this, you stinking cop. Uh, wait'll I get *you* trussed up, again, Kovary, you kinky son of a bitch! I swear to God, I'll beat your ass black and blue, before I fuck the hell out of it!"

"That's mighty big talk, coming from a guy who's got my slave boy's cock shoved up his ass," Emeric jeered. "Maybe, instead of all this mouthing off, you'd be better advised to try to talk Cordero into going easy on your ass."

"Fuck you, Cordero, and fuck you, Kovary! Aw, shit! Never should've let you perverts tie me up," Riley lamented.

"You wouldn't have any use for a *spark plug* right about now, would you?" Emeric inquired, mockingly. "Maybe a spark plug shoved up your ass?"

Riley bit his lip. "No—no, sir."

Emeric let out a snort of laughter. "Faker. What a faker! Pretending you don't like it, that you're not getting off on it. Well, you just had your chance to back out. Let him have it, Cordero. Fuck that ass."

"Too late for second thoughts or to set any limits now, dumbass," Cordero told Riley, callously. "I hope you're enjoying your slave status. You might as well. Because there's nothing you can do about it, now. Yee haw!" Cordero exclaimed. "I'm in the saddle and I'm taking a long hard ride. This is the kind of rodeo I like!"

"Pound that stud slave's ass." Emeric urged Cordero. "Own it!"

"Fuck, yeah!" Cordero agreed. "I'm going to get my dick deep in that hot hole."

"Ream it out. Go in *so* deep he'll think he's been torn right open," Emeric advised.

"Yes, sir!" Cordero cried.

He screwed Riley with monomaniacal concentration, while an obviously approving Emeric watched. Knowing that Emeric thought he was doing well excited Cordero almost as much as what he was doing to Riley. Writhing and cursing while he took the pounding, Riley must have thought that his ass hole would end up wrecked. He wasn't easily cowed, though. He spat out a steady stream of insults, telling the two tops exactly what he thought of them, including terrible speculations about their mothers' sex lives—which only made the sadistic studs guffaw at his expense, at first.

But then Emeric jacked up the roleplaying, pretending to be genuinely angry, and mean.

"Shut up and take that cock," he commanded. "That's enough out of your sewer mouth. Now, you *work* that ass of yours around my boy Cordero's dick. Squeeze it, bear down on it, just like you're taking a shit. Give him a real good ride.

Keep working your ass to make him feel good, or I swear to God I'll think up some *real* punishment for you. You'll be sorry you defied me, bitch."

Cordero was surprised and impressed by the fact that Riley didn't invoke his safe word. This was turning into some pretty rough play acting, which Cordero feared might get out of hand.

Doing a good job of looking terrified, thoroughly cowed, at last, Riley shut up, and he frantically employed every anal muscle which was under his voluntary control, in a desperate effort to keep his fucker satisfied.

"Oh, that's good," Cordero gloated. "That's so much better! What a number his ass is doing on my dick!"

Emeric grunted. "Funny, isn't it, how the fear of punishment can make a tough guy give it up?" he asked Cordero. "Aw, you know I wouldn't really hurt you, Riley," he told their prisoner, mock reassuringly. "No—I'd just slap you around a little, which I know damn well you actually kind of like. Or, better yet, I'd just take my nightstick and use it to tune you up a bit. Give you a good beat down with it, and then shove that baton right up your butt and fuck you with it. Give you the kind of reaming out that'll make you have trouble sitting down for a week! Still—don't you get too damn cocky. You'd better keep up that hot ass action, boy. Yeah, you'd better go on doing just what you're doing to keep Cordero happy, if you know what's good for you."

Riley went on doing just what he was doing, as he'd been told.

When Cordero did come, he completed his lurid domination fantasy by clamping his hand over Riley's mouth to stifle his cries. Thrusting his cock home with brutal abandon, Cordero shot off deep inside the other man, thoroughly breeding his ass.

"Your turn," Cordero told Emeric, breathlessly, yanking

his spent fuck tool out of Riley's butt. "Take him. Fuck him, cop. Fuck him good! I think the fight's just about been fucked out of him. He'll do whatever you want."

Emeric grunted. "He'd better," he responded, ominously.

Also eschewing lube, Emeric clasped Riley around the waist, and he pushed the head of his cock through his anal pucker and deep into his cum-filled ass hole. Riley grunted and squirmed, but after a moment, he thrust his behind into Emeric's groin, betraying his eagerness to feel another hot, hard cock inside him, stretching him, pounding his butt.

"How's that feel, you long-haired, inked-up freak?" Emeric taunted his victim.

"I hate your guts, cop!" Riley dared to say. "But I love your cock."

"Slut," Emeric responded, pithily.

"Ride him, cop," Cordero urged. "Ride him hard."

Riley groaned, "Oh, yeah. Give it to me. Give me all of that hot cop dick!"

"You're going to get it, boy. All the way up to the balls," Emeric promised.

"Oh, fuck me hard!" Riley begged. "Nail that ass of mine. Plow it hard and deep. Make me feel it, make it hurt. You lousy, stinking cop and your dirty, big-dicked college jock boyfriend. You guys are the roughest motherfuckers I've ever been with. God help me, but I like it. Sweet Jesus, forgive me, but I want to be fucked!"

"You'd better pray you don't piss off either of us," Emeric advised.

"Jesus can't save your ass," Cordero advised. "Your hole belongs to us, now."

Emeric snickered. "Good one, kid."

"I remember you saying something like that to me once, sir," Cordero told Emeric.

Emeric grunted. "You're an apt pupil."

Resigned, Riley bit on his lower lip, and Cordero, observing him, guessed that the guy did so to prevent himself from screaming his damn fool head off while Emeric screwed him. Cordero could easily put himself in Riley's place, imagining what the prisoner must be experiencing. Cordero wondered whether their willing victim would ever be able to contract his ass hole back to its normal dimensions again, once the two well-hung doms were done venting their lust on him.

Cordero offered Riley his cock, pressing it against his panting mouth.

"Here, this'll take your mind off that pain in your ass. Suck on that dick which was just up your ass, boy," Cordero coached him. "Taste your ass on it. Then my balls — take my balls in your mouth, both of them at the same time. Work on them while my partner reams out your ass."

Slavishly, abjectly, Riley obeyed. He did as he was told. But not under duress. Cordero could tell that he did it willingly, like the man whore he had become!

Emeric was clearly in the mood to hump hard and fast, holding nothing back, indifferent to the comfort or discomfort of the recipient of his thrusts. With a rapid, jerky pelvic action resembling that of a rutting jackrabbit, he continued to possess Riley's vulnerable butch ass.

The jarring rhythm of the fucking soon had Riley gasping, the sound muffled by the mouthful of balls which Cordero was force-feeding him. Riley seemed to be in the grip of a delirious blend of pain and intense sexual excitement. His cock shot off, spontaneously, without it having been touched, let alone stroked. The warm, slippery semen splattered over his inked pecs and abs.

A few minutes later, the hard-breathing, heavily-perspiring Emeric reached the point of orgasm himself.

"Aw, shit!" Emeric screamed. "Can't stand it. I'm either going to have to come, or die!"

"Come, officer, come," Cordero told him, heatedly. "Don't die! I can't afford to lose you! I couldn't live without that cop dick of yours!"

"Coming!" Emeric yelled, looking and sounding near hysteria in his climactic crisis. "Ah! The goddamn slave boy's sucking the cum right out of my cock!"

"Shoot! Shoot! Oh, shoot!" Cordero encouraged his sex-crazed mentor.

Riley's tattooed and pierced body writhed as Cordero pumped his fuck fluid into his rectum.

"Squeeze," Emeric demanded, gasping for breath. "Keep squeezing."

Cordero realized that Emeric was instructing Riley to tighten his anal muscles around the spurting cockshaft to prolong and intensify the pleasure for both of them, and to squeeze out every drop of Emeric's jism. Cursing, Emeric hammered his way through his ejaculation, and then he withdrew his emptied prick from Riley's well-used ass.

Only then did Cordero ease his testicles out of Riley's mouth.

"Okay," Emeric said, reluctantly, picking up the pocket knife. Observing him, Cordero saw that the storm of passion within him had ebbed away, leaving him drained — and in an unusually mellow frame of mind. "I guess we're going to have to cut you loose."

"Not yet," Riley pleaded. He was obviously enjoying being a prisoner. "First, *you* fuck me in my mouth, too."

"Maybe I'm going deaf, but I didn't hear you say *sir*, slave," Cordero chimed in. He was learning his lessons well. "I'd suggest you show your master, Officer Kovary, the proper respect, if you know what's good for you."

Riley shot Cordero an angry look, but he acquiesced.

"Please, Officer Kovary, sir, please fuck me in my mouth," Riley mumbled.

"That's better. Goddamn bossy bottoms," Emeric grumbled, as he moved to insert his cockhead between Riley's slavering lips. "Get ready to swallow a big load of cop cum!" he demanded.

Chapter Fourteen: In Unofficial Custody

"You did well." That was Emeric's assessment of Cordero's performance, when the two guys discussed their threesome with Riley. "Now you can take on either role, as you choose."

"I definitely want to top again. That was exciting as hell! But I have to admit it—I think I still prefer being the sub. You were right. I was able to put myself in Riley's place, imagine what was going through his head, while we worked on him. I was almost envious. Like I wanted all those things to be done to *me*."

Emeric smiled. "Empathy, as I said."

Emeric and Cordero were soon in the habit of getting together regularly for sex—sometimes one-on-one, sometimes inviting Bruce or Riley to join them.

Cordero always got off on the black cop's body, his cock, his ass—Cordero never failed to find him excruciatingly arousing, and satisfactory as a sex partner. But Bruce was almost exclusively a top. As for the versatile Riley, he harbored no grudges. Cheerfully, during their threesomes, he agreed to be either a top or a bottom, as the mood took him.

"You're crazy, Kovary," Riley told Emeric, after one particularly intense session, in which Riley once again bottomed. "As in *certifiably* crazy!" The way he said it, though, made it sound as though craziness was a good thing.

"Glad I was able to satisfy your ass," the cop retorted.

Cordero relished these adventures.

But Emeric was still Cordero's main man, the guy whom he preferred, whom he lusted after.

"We always get together at your place," Emeric remarked, the next time they were on the phone, making arrangements to hook up. "I don't want you to think I'm inhospitable. Why don't you come to my place this time, for a change?"

"Sounds good," Cordero replied.

"I'll give you the address."

Cordero wrote it down.

Cordero sensed that the invitation was yet another concession on Emeric's part, further acknowledgment that he had begun to think of Cordero as less of a subordinate and as more of an equal. Cordero had been curious about how his cop master lived. The apartment building was an older one, located in a once-neglected but now newly-gentrified neighborhood.

When Emeric let him into his apartment, Cordero saw that his host was in civilian attire—old faded jeans and a sweatshirt, padding about in his socks. He looked good like that, although for a moment Cordero *was* tempted to ask him to put on his uniform, just so they could play their favorite game of *arresting officer and perp caught in the act* again. Restraining himself, Cordero returned Emeric's smile, and they hugged and kissed.

Emeric offered Cordero wine, which Cordero accepted. Emeric had splurged on a Malbec, a quite good-quality vintage, and Cordero felt honored that he'd chosen to share it with him.

Maybe I'm more than just another casual trick to him, after all. I certainly hope so!

They sat and chatted while they drank.

"This is a nice place," Cordero remarked, sincerely.

"I like it. I'm comfortable here. It's my refuge, for me to hole up in, away from the stresses of work. I know that all cops like to bitch about how little they're paid. Doesn't everybody, no matter what he does for a living? But, to be honest, I draw a pretty decent salary. And the benefits are good. I can't complain. I should apologize, though, for my lousy housekeeping. The place is kind of messy, I know."

"Oh, I don't mind. My place is no better."

"Yeah, so I've observed," Emeric teased Cordero. "We're both slobs."

"I've got no one to complain about it and tell me to clean up. Neither do you, apparently. Don't you have a boyfriend, Emeric?"

"Me? A boyfriend? Hell, no."

"You say that as though having a boyfriend was something bad."

"It's all right for some, I guess. Personally—I like to play the field. Don't you? You're just a kid. At your age, a young guy, he's just coming out, and just starting to, you know, be gay. You're still going through what I call *the whore stage.* You want to have sex with as many different guys as possible. Oh, I'm not being critical, or judgmental. I've been there, done that, God knows. Fuck—maybe I'm still going through that stage. Stuck in it. But," Emeric added, with a sly, lewd grin, "I'm not at all penitent."

"Penitent—funny you should say that. Odd choice of word. I'm Catholic. Are you?"

"Well, I was raised Catholic. Not too observant, lately, I'm afraid."

"Guess you don't think being gay is a sin."

"Not at all. On the contrary. I think it's one of life's pleasures. And you? Feel guilty sometimes?"

"Not often, and not very."

"Good for you. Jesus! If you'll pardon the expression. I wasn't planning on getting into a theological or moral discussion with you, for Christ's sake! Aw, shit! There I go, blaspheming again," Emeric said, with a broad grin.

"I forgive you."

"Very good of you, boy."

They drank more wine, and they talked some more, affably enough.

But they were both eager to retire to the bedroom. At one point, Cordero stood up, and he wandered over to the living room windows, looking out to admire the view. Emeric had followed him, and they stood close together. Their conversation faltered, and they both fell silent.

From the first time they'd had sex, at his place, Emeric and Cordero had never been coy with each other. Neither of them had made any secret of the fact that he enjoyed sex. And so, when Cordero put his hand on the cop's butt, and he groped his ass cheeks through Emeric's tight faded jeans, and then he kissed him on the mouth, Emeric — to Cordero's delight — immediately seemed to recognize Cordero's move as an invitation to get the action going. Without saying anything more for the time being, Emeric took Cordero into his bedroom, where they got undressed.

Standing naked beside the police officer's bed, with their bare feet buried in the soft pile of the wall-to-wall carpeting, the two men fooled around a little, embracing and kissing, their hands roaming restlessly up and down each other's warm, aroused bodies, seemingly on their own.

Emeric was a good kisser, and Cordero always enjoyed sucking face with him. And he also enjoyed taking his cop master's cock in his hand and coaxing it into erection, because Emeric was hung so big, and he was so potent. It took very little stimulation to get him hard, to keep him stiff, or to revive his tumescence after he'd ejaculated once. Like a double-barreled shotgun, he was usually good for two blasts in close succession! After playing with his prick for a little while, Cordero finally got down on his knees in a posture of submission, and he licked Emeric's grossly swollen penis from its base to its tip, and then Cordero tickled his balls with his extended tongue.

Emeric's large testicles were coated with soft blond hairs. When both of his heavy, semen-laden nuts were matted and gleaming from Cordero's saliva, Cordero opened his mouth wide, and he sucked both balls inside.

As he drew on them gently with his lips, stretching the scrotum away from Emeric's groin, making Emeric tense up and moan above him, Cordero took the thick, stiff dick in his fingers again and he stroked it delicately — keeping Emeric excited, but being careful not to get him so aroused that he'd be in any danger of ejaculating prematurely.

"Fucking hell," Emeric groaned. "I ought to run you in for being such a goddamn tease! *That* should be against the law. My dick is as stiff as a board."

Cordero could empathize with him. Cordero's own erection was like a flagpole sticking outward from his groin. A flagpole, however, was an inanimate object, whereas his dick was very much alive, hypersensitive, hotly responsive to any kind of stimulation. After a few more intense minutes of ball-sucking and prick fondling on Cordero's part, Emeric put his hands on Cordero's shoulders, and he pushed him away from his crotch.

"Shit," he complained. "You've got me so damn hot. That felt so good! But I don't want to come yet!"

Breathing hard, he turned toward the bed, grabbed one of the pillows, and deposited it on the end of the mattress. Opening a drawer in his nightstand, he took out a strip of condoms and a plastic bottle of lube, which he tossed onto the bed. He stood by the bed, facing it, bending his knees slightly, and then he leaned over from his waist until his head, upper torso, and arms rested on the mattress.

The pillow cushioned his cock and balls, and his fine, big, hairy ass—the buttocks hard-muscled and round—stuck up in the air and back toward Cordero, a mute invitation to his lust. His message to Cordero couldn't have been clearer if he'd had the words *fuck me!* tattooed on the small of his back, with an arrow pointing down past his coccyx, toward his manhole.

But Cordero wanted to taste that hot cop ass hole before he fucked it.

He got down on his knees on the floor, grabbed hold of those enticing butt cheeks, and he spread them wide apart. Emeric let out a hiss of surprise and pleasure when Cordero buried his face in his ass crack, kissed his pucker, and penetrated it with his stiffened, wriggling tongue.

"Aw, hell, yeah!" the cop moaned. "Suck that ass!"

Hungrily, Cordero rimmed him, really getting off on the obscene oral-anal contact. Damn, the cop had a sweet ass! Cordero had to force himself to pull his mouth away from that juicy manhole. Reluctantly, gasping for breath, he stood up, and he let the head and the shaft of his aching prick rub over the upper curve of Emeric's enticing buttocks, just below his tailbone.

"Hurry, Cordero, you fucking goddamn stud," Emeric gasped. "Fuck me, kid! I'm really hot for it tonight!"

No surprise, there. He was always hot for it—and so was Cordero!

Cordero didn't hesitate or waste any time. Emeric was an incredibly talented fucker, who knew how to drive Cordero's ass hog wild with his cock. But Cordero knew he also loved to get fucked, Cordero loved screwing him, and this was a position they hadn't tried before.

Cordero tore one of the condoms off the strip, ripped the packet open, and put the rubber on, sheathing his phallic sword in the thin, translucent latex. Next, he squirted some of the lube onto his fingertips and massaged it over his rubber-ized dick. He deposited a second blob of the lubricant right between his cop lover's ass cheeks, pressing the slippery sub-stance through his sphincter muscle, adding it to the saliva which he'd just deposited there, and Emeric quivered with anticipation as Cordero finger-fucked him, none too gently.

"Quit screwing around," Emeric demanded. "Get that cock *in* me! And that's an order!"

"Right away, officer." Standing behind him, Cordero guided his latex-sheathed and well-lubed prick to its target, and he pushed it home, inserting it carefully, inch by inch, up his cop lover's wantonly suctioning ass hole. Emeric took him easily, already moaning with delight, and Cordero placed his hands on the man's restlessly squirming hips to steady him under him as he made his first fucking thrust deep into the horny police officer's spasming guts.

"Fuck me, fuck me! Oh, God, give me that dick!" Emeric howled.

"Take it, cop," Cordero told him, while he pounded his prick in and out of him.

"I'll take it, all right. All you've got to give!"

"Hot-assed cop. I ought to shove your nightstick up that horny butt of yours. I bet you'd be able to take the whole thing — and you'd enjoy it."

"You bet I would. But I wouldn't like it as much as I like your cock. You may not be as long as the baton, but you're thicker. Come on, Cordero, you goddamn young stud fucker," Emeric growled. "Is that all you've got? You're fuck-ing me like a pussy boy, like a punk. I want to feel that thing pounding in and out of me! Work that hole, you bitch!"

"You look like the one who's the bitch, bent over on your belly with your ass up and your hole plugged."

"Screw you — and screw me!"

"Great idea."

"Harder, motherfucker! Oh, do it harder!"

"Open up that cop cunt for me!"

"Fucker! Dirty, big-dicked Puerto Rican fucker!"

"Nasty hot-assed cop slut!"

"I never should have suggested that you give being the top a try."

"No, you shouldn't have. It's put all sorts of ideas into my head."

"Such as?"

"Such as having a big dumb Hungarian cop as my very own sex slave."

"Keep dreaming, bitch!"

"Tough guy, huh?"

"Punk, I can take anything you've got to give! And more!"

"Yeah? Let's find out. Take *that*, you big dumb bohunk!" Cordero spat out, accompanying his insult with an especially savage thrust into Emeric's ass.

"Uh! Fucker!" Emeric cried. "Shows how stupid *you* are. What's with the *bohunk* shit? For your information, that's a Czech."

"Same difference, isn't it?"

"You really ought to get a refund on your tuition money."

Cordero tried to think of an insulting term for Hungarian, but he failed to do so. All he could come up with was *Hun*, as in Attila.

"Stupid, am I, huh? Well, I'm smart enough to know how to pound your ass. Take it, Hun. Take it like the Hun whore you are."

"I'll take it, bitch, when you start fucking me like a real man, instead of just poking around in there with your pathetic little prick."

"Cop cunt!"

They goaded each other verbally like that, until Cordero's

overtaxed dick exploded inside the condom, inflating its reservoir tip like a tiny sperm-filled balloon jammed far up Emeric's squirming ass.

"Aw, shit!" Emeric squealed. "You're coming inside me, in my ass, aren't you, boy? I can feel it, your dick swelling — pulsing — unloading. Inside the frigging rubber, damn it! Jesus! I wish you were fucking me raw. Coming in me, with no condom to get in the way, to keep your jizz trapped. I wish you were breeding my ass!"

"Man, you sound like a girl getting fucked for the first time," Cordero taunted Emeric. "Like a dumb bitch, losing her cherry! Dude, could you be any more of a whiny little pussy, if you tried?"

"Whore — you boy whore — I swear to God, you'll pay — pay, for mouthing off to me like this!" Emeric vowed.

"Maybe, big man. Maybe not," Cordero, all insouciance, replied, airily. "Meanwhile, you seem to enjoy being fucked. Fucked like a cunt!"

After Cordero pulled out of him, Emeric rolled over onto his back on the bed, his legs hanging down over its edge, and he silently offered his erstwhile fucker his painfully swollen cock. Cordero took it in his right hand, and he beat it off for him.

While he slipped two fingers of his left hand up Emeric's relaxed, well-fucked ass hole, Cordero shuddered in empathetic lust and Emeric began to play with his own nipples, pinching them mercilessly, until he came in a hot white shower of cum which sprayed salty drops all over both men's bodies.

It was a safe sex act at its most intense, and both of the participants felt drained afterward. They lay there on the disordered sheets, cuddling.

"You fucker," Emeric murmured, his voice thick and indistinct with lingering sexual satisfaction.

"What's the matter, dude? You got any complaints?" Cordero challenged him.

"None at all. As a submissive, you're awfully damn good. As a dom, you're certainly getting there. Almost as good. Both things in one package. Maybe that's the problem."

"What problem?"

"I don't know, kid." Emeric sighed. "Sex is one thing. Getting all soft for a guy — falling for him — damn, that's another thing, altogether."

"What're you saying, cop?" Cordero demanded, aggressively. "Are you telling me you're getting soft for — falling for — *me?* You — the tough guy? The hard-assed cop?"

"Maybe," Emeric admitted, sheepishly.

"Well, then, why don't you man up and admit it? Own it?"

"I don't know. I'm embarrassed, I guess."

"More like you're afraid you'll seem weak, if you let yourself show any emotion," Cordero suggested.

"Maybe."

"Fuck that shit!" Cordero insisted. "Tell me, straight out. You want to be my main man, or not?"

"I want to be your main man."

"Okay," Cordero grumbled. "Don't see what was so damn hard about that."

"I kind of like that expression, *main man.* It's a little more nuanced than *top* or *master.* More accurate, when it comes to describing you and me. I love you, Cordero," Emeric said.

"Yeah? No kidding?" Cordero taunted him.

"No kidding. Come on, don't make me beg."

"All right, then," Cordero deigned to say.

"What about you? Do you love me, too?"

"I'm not indifferent to you," Cordero declared, in a studied, offhanded manner, trying his damnedest to look and sound blasé.

"Indifferent? Damn it! Is that all I can expect from you?"

Emeric exploded.

"Temper, now, temper, officer! Relax, big guy," Cordero told him. "Calm down, cop. Yeah — what the fuck. I guess I do love you, too." Feeling a need to lighten the mood, Cordero grinned at the indignant police officer, in his most ingratiating manner. "What can I do to prove it to you?"

Returning his grin, Emeric seemed more relaxed. "You can let *me* fuck *you*," he said.

"Payback time? Go right ahead, officer. Be my guest!"

Soon, like the man whore he was, Cordero was lying on his back on the bed, with his legs raised and resting on Emeric's shoulders, and his butt pressed firmly against the cop's crotch. Their bodies were joined together by Emeric's cock, which was sunk deep inside Cordero's ass. Willingly, Cordero threw himself upon the mercy of the law, so to speak. But this particular lawman wasn't showing him any mercy. And that thrilled him!

"Cop cock, damn it," Cordero growled. "Give me that cop cock! Let me feel it pounding in and out of my hole! Oh, fuck me rough, stud! You know that's the way I like it."

"What an ass," Emeric gloated. "You're so hot and tight — and you really know how to work that butt of yours! It's like a greasy fist jerking my dick!"

While he screwed Cordero, Emeric took his dick in his fist, and he masturbated him. He pumped savagely up and down on Cordero's prickshaft, all the while looking down at him, scrutinizing Cordero's face with lewd glee, gauging his reactions, aware of just how hot Cordero was making him. Emeric's manual efforts were suddenly rewarded, when the fat head of Cordero's well-fisted cock visibly pulsed, and then it spat out its charge of thick semen in a first awesome jet which rained big drops of cum all over Cordero's squirming, sweating torso. Cordero came so forcefully that the next spurt of his jism smacked him in the face!

"Now you," Cordero urged Emeric, heatedly, even while he was still ejaculating. "You shoot, too!"

"I'm right with you," Emeric groaned. "Yeah—here it comes—I'm going to blow!"

He came hard inside Cordero, grunting loudly with satisfaction, and then, letting go of Cordero's emptied prick, he touched him with both of his hands, running them over Cordero's face, his throat, his chest, his ribcage—caressing him with his outstretched, trembling fingers.

"Beautiful, boy! You are so fucking beautiful!" Emeric cried.

When he had stopped ejaculating, he sank down on top of Cordero, with his cock still jammed up his ass, and they kissed, passionately, with Cordero's slick sperm mashed between their bodies like an erotic lubricant.

Emeric got much more aggressive, pushing his tongue deep inside Cordero's open mouth and clutching his hair with his hand to keep Cordero's face close to his and their lips crushed together in breathless urgency.

"Mine, all mine," Emeric kept gasping, between their kisses. "You're all mine!"

His passion almost frightened Cordero, so intense was it.

Still, Emeric wasn't going to hear any arguments from Cordero. Cordero was his, all right. Any way his cop master wanted him! That would be fine with him.

Giddy with happiness, Cordero drew his cop lover down to him, pressing their bodies as tightly together as he could get them, while his lips sought Emeric's lips, again and again.

The End

You may also enjoy the following from eXtasy Books Inc:

A Thing for Cops
Roland Graeme

Excerpt

I've always had a thing for cops.

I've also always known I was gay — I mean, I've known it at least ever since I was old enough to get a hard-on. I suppose I was sexually precocious. From a young age and on, I was hot and horny, but I had no interest whatsoever in girls. All I ever fantasized about was men — their bodies, their crotches, their asses, their dicks. Especially their dicks. My jack-off sessions amounted to a form of phallic worship. Whenever I stroked my own agitated dick and coaxed it toward ejaculation, I fantasized devoutly about what it might be like to touch another guy's hard cock.

I was so young and dumb that I'd have been perfectly content just to touch one of those erections I pictured in my imagination. When I heard other guys making jokes about sucking cock and taking it up the ass, I was embarrassed. I couldn't believe that men — even gay men — actually did such things with each other. The whole idea was shocking to me.

As a result of my innocence and shame, I never had the

guts to try anything sexual with another guy until an opportunity arose that took me completely by surprise — not that I didn't take advantage of the chance and enjoy the experience when it finally happened. And it sure wasn't traumatic or anything like that. Hell, it was quite the opposite! Once I'd had my first taste of homosexual sex, I wanted to kick myself for not having indulged in it long before.

It happened shortly after my graduation from high school. That's a big milestone in any guy's life, of course. But in my case it paled in comparison to discovering my sexuality.

I was eighteen, not much of a scholar, but athletic. I was a big star on the football team — middle-class shit, which didn't cut much ice in the rough neighborhood I'd grown up in.

All during my four years of high school, I'd been such a good boy, so damn well-behaved, that it was probably inevitable I'd rebel a little, given the chance.

There was only a week to go before graduation. The teachers were already looking forward to the summer break, and they were much more relaxed and lenient than usual as a result. Needless to say, the students were "relaxed," too — to the point of being semi-comatose during school hours. They were coasting, counting the days. The big excitement was the upcoming prom.

Anyway, my life changed forever during one of those final days of my senior year. That sounds melodramatic, but it's no exaggeration. At school during lunch hour, I was in the men's room taking a long, leisurely piss, just minding my own business but half tempted to get my cock hard and whack off right then and there to relieve my constant frustration. If I slipped into one of the toilet stalls and took care of business, who would ever know?

Then the door opened and in walked, or rather strutted, Marco Torelli, one of the really rough neighborhood kids, the kind your mother warns you not to associate with. All sorts of lurid stories circulated about Marco. Supposedly, he smoked pot and busted chicks' cherries for them and got them knocked up, and he carried a switchblade—all that sort of thing.

And he was a good-looking young stud. He had muscles out to here, and a sexy punk face. He always looked as though he needed a shave.

I'd always made a point of steering clear of him. Now, I was scared shitless at the mere coincidence of finding myself alone in the men's room with him. I thought he might grab me and beat me up right there in the john, just for the hell of it, or at least shake me down for money the way he did with younger kids all the time. "Pay up or get slashed, punk," was the usual way he put it, according to some of his victims who'd confided in me about their confrontations with him.

But Marco didn't react to my presence in the toilet at first. He glanced around the john to make sure that we were alone, just the two of us. That certainly didn't make me feel any more confident.

Then he kind of swaggered toward me—I was still standing at the urinal, pissing—with this big grin on his face, his hands stuck in his pockets, his crotch packed with fat cock meat and shoved out toward me. It was a real come-on act, although I was still too young and dumb to recognize it as such at the time.

He came up to the urinal right beside mine, unzipped his jeans, and pulled out the biggest prick I'd ever seen. Needless to say, Marco wasn't on the football team, so I'd never had the chance to check out his equipment in the locker room or anything like that. So I was completely unprepared for what I now saw.

To my awe, he was giving me one hell of an eyeful of man-sized cock. It was still soft, but already getting noticeably stiffer. He hefted it up in his hand to aim it at the urinal and gave himself a little squeeze, looking me right in the eye with that lewd, suggestive grin of his.

"How's it going, man?" he asked me.

"Okay, I guess."

"Being stuck in here in classes all day sucks, doesn't it?"

"Yeah, it sure does."

"Thank the fuck there's less than a week to go."

"Yeah," I mumbled.

"Hey, do you want to hang out for a while, after school?"

I spoke on pure instinct, without thinking. "Sure."

Marco told me to meet him at a certain coffee shop, downtown. Stunned, I agreed.

I was so surprised by the fact that he'd actually spoken to me, let alone that he wanted to spend some time with me, that it didn't occur to me to ask him exactly what he had in mind, besides coffee.

But I kept our rendezvous. I lied to my parents, of course. I called them and told them I was going over to a friend's house to study with him for a couple of hours. They were so proud of me — toiling away at my studies, right up to the end!

Marco showed up promptly at the coffee shop. He was carrying a small gym bag, which he set down on the floor beside our table while we sipped our brews and talked.

"Who're you taking to the prom?" he asked me.

"No one."

"What, are you going alone?"

"I'm not going at all."

"Why not? Don't tell me you couldn't find a date."

I shrugged. "I'm just not into the whole prom thing. Proms are so middle class."

Marco grunted. "What's wrong with being middle class? Look at me. I'm barely one step above trailer trash. Middle class would be a move upward for me."

"So who are you going to the prom with?"

"Oh, I'm not going, either. I can't be bothered. With my luck, I'd end up getting my date pregnant." He sipped his coffee, then gave me a wry look over the rim of his paper cup. "So tell me how the other half lives," he said.

"Huh?"

"Tell me what it's like to be a big stud jock and have all the younger kids look up to you—and all the teachers respect you." He gave the word respect a wry inflection that made it sound like a dirty word.

"Aw, give me a break. They don't do that. I just like to play football, that's all."

"I bet that's not all you play. I bet you get plenty of pussy."

"Not so much," I said. I was trying not to blush, which might betray the fact that I wasn't getting any.

"I bet you have cock suckers chasing after you all the time, too."

"No." Now I could definitely feel my face getting hot. "I don't even know any cock suckers."

Marco laughed. "Sure you do."

He proceeded to name two of our classmates and one of our teachers. I was stunned.

"They're gay?" I asked.

"Hell, yes."

"How do you know?"

He shrugged. "How do you think?"

By now I was feeling marginally less intimidated in Marco's presence. "I suppose you have first-hand knowledge," I dared to taunt him.

He met my gaze without flinching, and he kept the same expression of mild, detached amusement on his face. "Maybe I do—and maybe I don't."

"Well, I definitely don't."

"Actually, I didn't think you had," he replied—whatever he meant by that. "Hey, you ready to go?"

"Sure."

I was surprised to see Marco stash his empty paper coffee cup inside his gym bag. I wanted to ask him why he was saving it, but I felt tongue-tied. I didn't know him well enough yet to begin asking him a lot of direct, personal questions.

Nor did I ask him where we were going. I followed him outside and down the block without question, like a stray dog trotting along at a pedestrian's heels.

But we didn't walk far. On the corner was an old office building. It had an abandoned, rundown look in general, and its exterior could have used some cosmetic work. A big sign announced that the location offered Prime Furnished Office Spaces for Lease.

Marco led me around to the back of the building, where a steel door was marked Deliveries. To my surprise, he pulled out a key and unlocked the door.

"Don't just stand there," he told me. "Come on."

ABOUT THE AUTHOR

Roland Graeme is a prolific author of erotica, who has also published classical music criticism.

www.ingramcontent.com/pod-product-compliance
Lightning Source LLC
Chambersburg PA
CBHW060825120626
46557CB00001B/370